From The Wom
34 Great Sutton Street, London

Lucy Anne Watt has worked as a schoolteacher, for advertising and film production companies, in newspaper and magazine offices. She now runs her own small business in Dorset, within sight of the sea. She has published several short stories; a selection of her poetry appeared in *Chatto New Poets: Number Two* (1989), and her short story, 'Thinking of Evans' was published in *Reader, I Murdered Him* (The Women's Press, 1989).

MICAWBER'S AILMENT

Lucy Anne Watt

The Women's Press

First published by The Women's Press Limited 1992
A member of the Namara Group
34 Great Sutton Street, London EC1V 0DX

British Library Cataloguing-in-Publication Data
Watt, Lucy Anne
  Micawber's ailment.
  I. Title
  823.914 [F]

  ISBN 0-7043-4287-1

Typeset by Contour Typesetters, Southall, London
Printed and bound by BPCC Hazell Books,
Aylesbury, Bucks, England

'My other piece of advice, Copperfield,' said Mr Micawber, 'you know. Annual income twenty pounds, annual expenditure nineteen nineteen and six, result happiness. Annual income twenty pounds, annual expenditure twenty pounds ought and six, result misery. The bloom is blighted, the leaf is withered, the god of the day goes down upon the drear scene, and – and in short you are for ever floored. As I am!'

Charles Dickens, *David Copperfield*

1

My advice is, never do tomorrow what you can do today. Procrastination is the thief of time. Collar him!

February 1989

'The first thing to go,' Napoleon Burnes said, 'is the sense of ordinariness.'

But *which* ordinariness? Elisabet imagined several. Take Napoleon's. It was material in nature; he was a man whose substance was measured by his relationship with things. They were ordinary things for the most part, rejects too. But in the scrubbed light of his last room – from which they put him, like a cat, into the street – in the light which never shone but sometimes rested in a grainy torpor on bricks he had whitewashed himself, Elisabet could not think of Napoleon but as lifting up or laying down, or gathering or depositing, or moving from or to – though it might be only a knitted scarf or his chipped lemony cup, sides glacial as sorbet, or the handle of the emaciated broom, which shed its hairs pitifully each time it was used and then, after, in brindled clumps, stood slyly by the back door as if pleading to be put from misery. All Napoleon's possessions were dispirited, woebegone, but at the same time dignified, made extraordinary by the way he used them to gauge, to evaluate his position.

His plight reminded Elisabet that each time you lose something, what is left increases in value. Napoleon, on the threshold of the streets before Elisabet, had a dog-like attachment to his old pieces. The puppy, equally, with an old blanket or chewed shoes, or the alcoholic dosser, with his collapsible coffin and blood-tepid spirits, feels something approaching symbiosis, the psyche of each cherished article capable of rising or bedding with its master and, at intervals, suckling his mongrel spirit.

In the end, in the last week before his homelessness, Napoleon had moved with the tenderness of a curator between objects of great rarity; and that the torn leatherette seat from an early Cortina could act as throne, and visibly ennoble when he sat there, was due as much to his fear as his love. He would not have, when they evicted him, even a lavatory and so, more cherishable than the burgundy settee (which could only, sadly, be spray-waxed or sponged), his last sanitary requisite was kept sweetened by the bleach bottle and the black plastic of the incomplete seat glossed. Elisabet, using it, felt her eyes pricked by caustic perfumes and an aura of holiness, enhanced by a bunch of tiny prayer bells, sensitive as wind chimes, and almost as busy, attached to the toilet-roll holder.

Later, when she bought Napoleon a coffee at a take-away-or-eat-in off the Embankment, it was not illness which made his hands shake as he told her about ordinariness. He had now a bedroll and a larder in a bin liner, and unfragrant garments, more like heaps of wool and fibre, which you would not think fit to clothe a body, stuffed in a white plastic supermarket carrier whose logo, claiming title to goods (Napoleon's) which it had never purveyed, nor would wish to purvey, was an irony lost on neither of them. This bogus adherence epitomised, to Elisabet, the sort of pain (though some are smaller, many greater) those without endure.

'You wouldn't know, until you haven't, that things matter so much.'

Napoleon tried to smile at her with long, doomed teeth, some of which had already gone. Hair, which grows when it should not, and vice versa, quickly discovers a lack of means to cut and groom. Napoleon's thin, brownish locks had shot, since their last meeting, from ear lobes to coat collar, though he must have taken something to the feathery, uneven fringe above his brows which stirred with the air disturbed by his nodding.

'When you say ordinariness' – Elisabet was

3

being careful with her words, because she did not want to upset him more than he already was – 'and if you don't feel that, though I don't know exactly what you do mean by that, what *do* you feel?'

Napoleon could not understand her attempt at casuistry, but he could see that he had a choice of questions, and could select which one to answer. It was important to Elisabet that he find the words to fit his experience: some day, and perhaps that day was not too far off, she would have to find a vocabulary for herself. A method, that was, of arranging her emotions around what had gone, in a way that would be the least painful, least brutal. Recovery, or acceptance – if there can be acceptance – to some extent depends on *which* words you choose.

She hoped that, for herself, there would be something else to describe, to shape and govern, something coming out of that loss which looked pretty inevitable – a loss through which she saw drawn, as into some kind of vortex, all the possessions contained, but barely contained, by her bedsit in Victoria. Goods, to her, currently seemed as valuable as looking-glasses: stored with memories, they gave back always. Yet they were more constant than mental data, their references exact. She could not imagine them fulfilling an equal role when stowed in plastic bags in a supermarket trolley. She could not see how, on a windy pavement, you would need them so much.

Is that what Napoleon meant by the ordinariness going?

Napoleon now held his paper cup of coffee with great delicacy. That this was a rare treat moved Elisabet so that her eyes filled and she had to bend her head to conceal their overflow. Not quite successfully: one tear ran with hot shame into her neck. A man who cannot put on his own kettle, and draws water from a tap cheek by jowl with his own sanitary arrangements, has had everything taken away. Napoleon's tenderness in his kitchen, and his childish delight in the etiquette of spoon and cups, had seemed to her, strangely, the index of his masculinity. A borrower now, an odorous man relying on favours – depending, for instance, on tolerance to sit in a public place, to hire a stool among the sweeter people of the café – becomes not only pathetic but desexed. What is left then is private anatomy, or deliberate churlishness, such as she had seen on the part of his neighbours, sucking on the teats of spirit bottles to prove in a roundabout fashion that they were still male.

'It's like,' Napoleon said, choosing the latter half of her question to answer, 'every morning looking for yourself. They wake us awfully early, with cleaning carts and hoses – as if we didn't feel dirty enough. And you're awake, and cold – I can't tell you how sore and cold – and not believing, you know, that this person who must do this, and whom you are watching, as if it is a play, that this person is one and the same with yourself.'

He shook his head slowly, making the hair flap.

'No, it's not possible. You cannot have accepted it, I mean.'

Elisabet nodded in sympathy, and made a stab, past her own dread, towards the practicalities to which she had so far managed to cling. These hedged her disbelief; she did not yet fully understand that it was possible to fall below the safety net of care she had always thought of as an ethical value. If government did not encompass the practice of being good neighbours, encompass it by policy, she meant, then what did government in a democratic state mean? That Napoleon was here, living in shifting, open situations, without a roof over his head, without facilities, and others like him, and herself horribly on that margin too, was an oversight, surely, that diligence could redress?

She thought quickly of her father, of home, family, and empire-shoring practices of taxes, rates and church. When she thought like this, and of the indented pair of islands, with their froth of smaller islands, whose continuity had been so important during the wars, and whose

Punch and Judy profiles on her classroom walls
remained unassailed by pins (she could just
remember this) while the bulk of Europe blistered
with an embarrassing, multicoloured eczema –
when she thought of certain facts and rituals
which were established then, she thought in
terms of picture postcards, or set scenes; she
thought in terms of firmness and tidiness. 'Everything in its place.' Her mother's maxims applied
as much to morals as to things. Her childhood's
dictums had been as solid as the house, post-
Great War, in which they had lived, as the
almost visible pillars supporting their lives: the
home and family; religion; work.

And there was the town and the countryside –
these were also distinct. They travelled between
one and the other. The countryside was soft and
usually wet, blue, grey and green; while an
oyster-bronze coast was reserved for the sharper
weather of summer. The city was stone and
soot-coloured, harsh, noisy but, incredible to
believe now, *safe*.

Elisabet sighed. Memories were ineffective
salves in times of trouble. On the contrary, they
became a pain in themselves, as if through
rigorous scrutiny they might, as they often
threatened, give up the reasons why she had
come to this, down to this, while at the same
time reminding her of decades of gradual attri-
tion. It was nearly true that, as her father had

feared, Elisabet had only the gift of perpetual childhood. As an adult (at least, as far as authorities were concerned) she had, in an infantile, irresponsibly non-learning fashion, failed to manage.

Or almost, because she had not quite reached that state. She hung on, had her room, books, clothes, cups, beads, combs, a bunch of lavender statice, a telly, a Bakelite radio which still worked, drawers jammed with personal greyish-yellow much-mended, nylon and cotton, embroidered cushions, a cushion made from a faded, goat-smelling rug, four decades of diaries and assorted writings, shoe-boxes of letters, mats of hand-crafted lace, two teddies worn to a shine, six, or was it seven, pairs of shoes, a belt with rhinestone buckle, more belts (she was fond of belts – they did a lot for a drab dress), how many belts? Elisabet's possessions, making a swift, sharp, elaborate contrast with the paucity of Napoleon's, passed through her memory's eye as quickly as a needle will turn once, twice, in the light as it is dropped. To Napoleon she seemed only to blink – she must have been thinking for a minute, because she was silent.

But the genesis of her thought was not lost, while it graved very deep lines in her face. Napoleon knew of the Mrs Ramsay of the Skye beaches, and thought Elisabet even more beautiful. It seemed incomprehensible to him that a

person with such a gift for, and of, bounty should
be in danger of being displaced. Neither could he
understand – though Elisabet had emphasised it
many times – that she felt not Ramsay-like but
the opposite: unmaternal, foolish, just marginally
more assertive than her friend. There seemed to
be a great disparity between how you looked
when mature and how close and real you felt
your irresponsibility was.

'You're scared, E.,' Napoleon said (he liked to
shorten her name – its full version diminishing
the grandeur of his own) when he realised she
was gathering up the beginning of her thought.
He could tell this much from old acquaintance.
Elisabet was always punctilious about looping
back to the start, no matter how long or
intriguing the thread she had been diverting
herself with. Napoleon knew he was not alone in
envying Elisabet her thoughts.

'No.' Her mouth acquired the firmness which
indicated she was 'taking things on'. Compressed
straightness did not suit it. 'No, not that.' A bit of
a lie – but still.

'It's something else. Napoleon, I am going to
have another go at having something done for
you. There *must* be a route.'

Instant sadness flooded Napoleon's face, and
he dipped his head so far that he would not be
looking at the top of his cup but at the table's
edge. Elisabet had seen the look before, an

end-of-the-line, don't-let's-bother-further look,
indicating, as Napoleon clearly thought, that it's
almost safer, and certainly less demeaning, to be
absolutely out of everything than to be still
within the reach of an indifferent and not very
tractable net. In a sense there is status in being a
bum. That has a name. The other words used
always sound like *scrounger*, and confer less
desirable, because less whole, identities. How
odd that there should be more dignity in being
penniless than in being merely poor.

'You mustn't give up.'

She could not pat his hands, which were under
the table, probably clenched in his lap, so she
patted the table on his side instead.

'Hostels?' Napoleon's voice had the double
handicap of its place of origin, almost on a level
with the table, and his difficulty in using it.
Elisabet thought she detected a question. And
then, a short burst of words, all of them
undistinguishable, save the last: ' . . . won't!'
Doubtless that word sufficed.

Elisabet's hand, still extended, patted the
table again.

'I think we must have overlooked something,'
she said hurriedly. She had not forgotten that
something nightmarish had happened to Napoleon
once, in a Sally, but that kind of temporariness
was not what she intended.

She could see how he much preferred to be

shifting under the stars, however cold, rather than in a succession of dorms where stench, aggression and latched doors increased his vulnerability.

'Anyway, we'll see.'

The motherliness in her tone jarred. Just fifty, or fifty and a bit, the half-hundred seemed an abstract, inapplicable to herself. It was true that it represented the comparison between her birth date and the present, yet it seemed to her that it was less chronology than mental age (a quite different mathematics) which mattered. Some politicians, for instance, were always, in that part of the brain where intellect contorts as well as avoids certain experiences, too limited, too old. They had gone so far beyond the possibility of encountering certain conditions that they were sure these things either never happened or, if they were unlucky enough to witness them, would, as the Persian monarch's rings assert, pass smoothly away. As smoothly as their eight-cylinder cars purred past the homeless grouped round churches, stations, and railway arches, whose very exposure, whose huddling like sheep under harsh arc lamps, must appear as naïve as those who, with soup runs, prayers and clothing donations, attempt to assuage part of the apparent tip of the iceberg of their problem. Better, almost, to leave it alone.

Then there was employment's index of full

maturity. It was her view that employment should not be expected of everyone, from and to a certain age, as if all had the mentality required for undertaking it. Elisabet had been a disastrous employee, and latterly no one wanted to have her. This applied as much to Napoleon as, she believed, to those sleeping alongside him – wherever he slept. They had all, she often thought, always been too ingenuous to operate the systems of petty lies and anomalies required at places of work. Also, they had been without ambition or, at least, the ruthlessness required to make ambition operate, so they had never risen to posts of responsibility (responsibility which they would never have been able to apply) and had, inevitably, grown bored with the more menial tasks they were allotted.

Over the years, these failures would be compounded. And for those innocents unlucky enough not to have a talent for performing (as in theatre, arts, crafts, or hippiedom – once it was self-sufficiency, small-scale, goat-based farming, etc., but that, requiring capital and commitment, was more financially tricky), for those like herself and Napoleon, without a particular talent able to attract fulfilment and pennies, there was no place. There is a close link between repeating humdrum work in different locations and not wanting to do any work at all; this, actually, is sometimes the same thing as not being *able* to do it. Surely anyone could see – Elisabet raised her eyebrows over the edge of the up, making Napoleon, who was lifting his head up, smile – that where we *can*, we *do*. It is only cheaper, not wiser, to pretend the opposite.

But she had been drifting again . . .

'Look,' she said, holding out her right wrist. 'It's nearly lunchtime.'

Napoleon tried to look diffident but looked only hungry. That was the saddest look that Elisabet had ever seen him achieve. Her mind drew a firm, indelible circle round it: Napoleon's long face, already much greyer, inclined towards her, while outside she could see, squatting against an indeterminate warehouse, three men passing a Bell's bottle from hand to hand. One had the standard plastic carrier at his feet, white, a replica of Napoleon's, and the wind made a bizarre show with their buttonless jackets and trousers, forcing them, like sails, the maximum or most fastidious distance from wasted limbs. Beyond, by straining her neck from their window seat, she could just see the descent where the arches of Hungerford Bridge rise and move to their vanishing point, a cruel blank under which the dirty river curdled. London, to these men, was obviously as distant and callous as the cold shorthand for it on the opposite shore, an embattled skyline, like a row of teeth

13

with caries, from which Napoleon had delicately turned away, his opposition creating the last touch to the picture now marked by her mind. She would remember it, she thought, for ever.

Napoleon, however, had other ideas. Catching her eye, he glanced at the clock on the wall, a determined move, almost desperate: of course, he was concerned with the uncomfortable present, and the fact that the greasy clock read just after twelve. Elisabet, who had already reminded him of the hour, was obliged to carry her responsibility through and buy Napoleon another cup of coffee, a frazzled bacon and tomato sandwich, and a small, dry doughnut, the same for herself. This was lunch. She had known, on starting out, that it was to be the day of the widow's mite. She was resigned, therefore, even to the quality of the food, as pulpy and tasteless as it was unduly expensive – though Napoleon seemed to make his meal sumptuous, almost festive, being silent while he constantly altered the relationship of the pieces, as if they were the subjects of some restless Picasso collage which was not to be consolidated until it was consumed.

Another hard thing for Elisabet's friend was that, without a home, he had nothing to do. Bereft of the interplay between himself and his belongings, the confiding presence of a sofa, table, kettle, and the many small variations of movement and lack of movement which can be carried out around, between, or perched on these objects, with the help of a book, or a newspaper, or a cup of tea, he came out into the street with her and looked as he felt – utterly lost.

Poor, poor Napoleon. She meant this in the genuine sense of the adjective. Where would he sit, what would he do? Patently, he wanted to come with her. But if he came, she could do little for him, because his presence was an encumbrance. Napoleon had even less patience than she did for council offices, for the bleak waiting-rooms of benefit departments, and the frustrating blank walls met at the end of interminable, in-depth questioning. Not even Napoleon could remember where he had last worked (it was very many years ago) and what he had earned, or what authority had last supported him. He could not remember his national insurance number, or even that he had ever had one; nor could he ever bear in mind (a point worth bearing in mind) that if he acted spontaneously, acted on his own initiative, a penalty often ensued. This was usually the condition on which the door, part-open during hours of questioning, was slammed in his face. Elisabet was sure that the government officers knew, before they started out, the reason why they would stall his claim for more help. But she had read Kafka, among others, and understood that interrogators enjoy their job. The sessions are much more entertaining if, having dangled a little bait before the interviewee, you withdraw it at the end. They had, then, no wish to come up with the trump question first, because that would rob them of at least half an hour's pleasure.

(Yet she did not blame the individuals. To judge by their faces, they regarded themselves as bored ciphers; even the joy obtained from what Elisabet considered malpractice was a machine-made joy, less theirs than – like the bully's – part of an established canon, a system which had just, in Napoleon's case, cruelly saved itself a penny or two.)

'What was your last address, Mr Burnes?'

It was a simple question, but Napoleon had forgotten the answer as soon as he was dispossessed, and Elisabet actually had to visit the squat – a tedious journey – because she had never written to him there, (besides, all his papers were lost) and only knew house and street by sight. Answers were made harder by the fact that the building, part of a condemned terrace, had long ago lost its number, or any other form of identity.

Poverty is fatiguing, that is certainly true. And if, as in her case, you can neither afford nor face long sessions in ill-smelling phone booths, then you must visit all the services in person. You must catch buses, or walk dismal streets between bus and tube stops, and spend very long hours in waiting-rooms, rooms in which, among the other people sitting there, all vestiges of well-being or confidence have been forgotten. And the dredging up of the same dull information is additionally fatiguing: the process erodes, de-identifies. With each detail conceded, more privacy slips away. Sometimes it is hard even to surrender the secret, personal tag of first as well as surname, because this offers the interviewer, and whoever else reads the file, that password or code by which a safe world may be entered, movements documented, anonymity cancelled. Names are almost as potent as toenails and hairs, while to turn out other details – financial, medical, marital (details the better-off regard as highly private) – is almost like undressing in public, or offering the body – its inside, rather – to the indifferent, analytical eye of the surgeon.

After each session on her own or Napoleon's behalf, Elisabet felt violated, humiliated. She felt, in short, raped.

Lunch over, she bought her friend a newspaper and settled him, in a weak ray of sun, in the Embankment Gardens. Now he wore newspapers under his jumpers (it was early spring, chilly) and crackled when he moved. Also, he smelt. Elisabet moved off quickly, wanting to cry.

Her first call should be the benefit office in Southwark, to which, after a delay caused by Napoleon's inability or repeated disinclination to find them, and the subsequent lapse of his claim, his papers were being passed. Having drifted out of the catchment area of the old office, he had imagined, and no one had offered to tell him otherwise, that his entitlement to support had passed. Elisabet had had not only to nag, cajole, intervene, but also to lend, which meant here, to give.

The trail to Keyworth Street would have been bad enough even if her spirits had not already reached rock bottom. Another encounter with the intricacies of the social security system could hardly sink them any lower. She knew too well what the effect would be this afternoon, like turning a stiff key in the door of a condemned cell. For although, only an hour before, one had felt (as countless times, even at bedrock level) here was depression but there, close by (she did not know exactly where), was escape – the effect, after that, was to know only the depression and to see no remedy.

The step between hope and its opposite is a short, dramatic, sometimes fatal one. *One should never forget that*, Elisabet said out loud, thus confessing her loneliness to those who looked as she veered suddenly north of the river, turning her back on the point where, at the water's edge, the brisk merchandising, the inflations of the West End, are cut off as, allegorically, they might be in Bunyan. At the Embankment, they were already at a low ebb: to the depth of just one street, up to the Strand, cheap tawdry goods, more properly belonging to the metaphorical divide, had seeped up, attracting some alcoholics who were, poor men, at night probably pavement fellows of Napoleon. Seeing here, with a stab of dread, his next stage – he wasn't strong enough, his powers of resistance feeble – Elisabet hurried, climbing Villiers Street and skirting Trafalgar Square by way of the National Gallery, where she wondered about paintings, but no, she wouldn't, not this afternoon. Even though they immeasurably cheered her, she had Napoleon to think of (though it would be easier not to think of him; we do not want to think of, to admit another's misery). After some minutes she turned into Charing Cross Road.

The next best thing to paintings, and sometimes better, because you can own them, are books. Here, in the second-hand markets, is true democracy. (She did not include rare books.) By this she meant that owning a duplicated, used example of the best of writing can cost very little: the maximum it costs, in comparison with other solids – a couturier outfit, a sofa, even, nowadays, a cup and saucer – is £2 or £3. Even Elisabet could afford the odd dog-eared paperback, had at home shelves of wisdom – cream and orange, vanilla and green Penguins, and the later black shiny Classics, Aristophanes, Maupassant, Herodotus, books she hadn't actually read cover to cover, but liked to look at, read a paragraph or two in, sometimes.

And then Elisabet thought, browsing at a rack of pastel-bound thrillers in Quinto's, there was this facelessness about reading, this not mattering who you are. The poor dropping in on the fictional lives of the wealthy and vice versa. You could read Bunyan nude and it did not matter, because only the ability to absorb, to understand, counted.

Only she did not like oil sagas, brand-name books, books about getting and having and the supposed discomforts, dramas of that milieu. *Their* pains were muffled, cushioned, infuriating to Elisabet because such traumas cannot hurt, are not capable of hurting, deeply, ineradicably, like hers. Wouldn't we all like safety nets, bought comforts, material medicine when we fall? And wouldn't we all, as a consequence, as fiction would have it, be then – because there is so little to fear really – even more adventurous and brave?

By now Elisabet had reached the noisy

junction with Shaftesbury Avenue, and turned to walk back down, browsing for the second time. She would buy something. She had £11.37 to last until the end of the week (it was only Tuesday) and, strictly speaking, if she spent £1 minimum on a book, she would have to do without something; yet all her purchases were vital, carefully balanced, until her giro cheque came. On the other hand, Napoleon's losses, his current critical loss of a home, had created in her an enormous need for having. She almost *had* to buy, in order to compensate for what he had not – as if his lack was a contagion, a corrosive leprosy, against which she must be armed. She spent a long time choosing and, in the end, unable to decide between two books, thick paperbacks with attractive covers, bought both.

The bill was £3.70, which meant that, until Friday, she must cut more than one corner in her expenditure – a not particularly depressing thought. Or not yet. She had the vague idea – not a new one, because poverty breeds ideas like this, few of which turn out to be feasible – that next week she would make up for the inroads. It was the old Wilkins Micawber problem, a belief in 'something turning up' never really going away. How could it? That would be like, in winter, forever precluding the sun.

It was now a great deal colder, the clouds having

21

lowered and darkened, and she hurried the short distance to Great Newport Street, where, at the health food restaurant, she bought a restorative cup of Earl Grey tea, with a fragrance suggesting homoeopathic medicine – an evocation of better times – and a slab of rough-textured cake which, broken open, spilled out small filaments of carrot. These cost another £1.30. But she was under the impression she always was before money changed hands and her purse grew light – here small change is a bare-faced liar, its weight belying its worth – that her purchases were essential.

She sat for over half an hour, relishing the spicy perfume of the beverage. The cup was thick, with a treacly glaze, awkward to drink from, but Elisabet had, in its place, conjured up a light porcelain dish-shape, with small grey print on the medallion at its base, saying something like Worcester or Spode or Crown Derby, and around her a tearoom with the cosy furnishings of the mid-fifties, the sort of place she had often visited, albeit rebelliously, with Mother, in her first durable suits and the two rows of real pearls she had never imagined she would regret. How old had she been? Mid-teens, with the naïve idea that you could always regain security if you wanted.

Today she had no choice but to eat her carrot cake as if it were thin bread and butter, wishing all the time there was a pot from which to draw more tea. Mother had paid the bills in the dainty teashops, neither of them imagining there would come a time when Elisabet, alone in London, could run only to snacks in funny cramped little bars, where you sat, in an aura of grease, almost on top of your neighbours. And these for treats, special, splendid treats, while a tea which came on a tray, with hot-water jugs, in a pretty room where they played music and provided chintzy cushions as part of an attention she now never had, was out of her range. In London it cost something like £3 to have a tea like that – excluding extras, even thin bread, and a contribution for the indifferent service.

Three pounds at the moment was one tenth of all her week's money, all her cash after the rent was paid. While the average weekly wage, she had been given to believe by a piece in the paper, should now be well over £200.

Towards closing time, during her last call in Liberty's, Elisabet remembered Napoleon. She had bought herself a pallid cooked quiche from Marks and Spencer, and some slender, translucent carrots, as light as lady's fingers – a pound for £1.20, yet she felt so short of aesthetic content, she *must* be able to afford them. Tonight, because she *deserved*, she would eat like a lady, not yet thinking of how much it would cost to heat her tiny oven in order to warm the quiche. It was unpalatable cold (she had tried it – it tasted as she imagined wet papier mâché does) and besides, cold food was for the end, the bitter outdoors end, which she had not yet reached. Until that, Elisabet would cling to the tail end of her dignity.

In this spirit, she also acquired a bar of rich dessert chocolate from a small specialist shop, tempted by the smooth beige and brown design and luxurious gilded touches on the packet. It was a limited edition, non-ubiquitous article; it would not taste like a Cadbury or Rowentree – indeed, it cost a great deal more and she would feel, again, treated as she ate it. But first she intended to let it sit somewhere prominent in her room, where the packet's distinction could pass as a present. Presents had become another practical demonstration of her state, growing proportionately scarcer as the inability to give them increased.

In Liberty's, Micawber's ailment manifesting uncomfortably, she also succumbed. Not extravagantly, although the patterned lawn handkerchief, covered with small pink rosebuds on a ground of grey and greenish-grey leaf, a sort of portable garden for the gardenless, had cost £1.70, so that now she had just over £3 left in her purse. Suddenly, the broken £5 note, the modern antonym of loaves and fishes, had dwindled to almost nothing, to £3 until Friday! This would not matter so much if there was food at home, and if it wasn't so cold (journeying between shops, she had noticed a new edge to the wind) and if she hadn't . . .

It was here, in the notions hall of Liberty's, just after her purchase, caught out in a flagrant act of self-indulgence (or theft – whose? – for money, too much, had changed hands) that she remembered Napoleon. In one way, it was very hard to believe in him, and the guilt his memory provoked. It was hard because here was visible, tangible superfluity. There (she was not exactly sure where, at this hour) the next stage to nothing. While being jostled continuously by people in furs and very well-made coats, by people very free with leather and perfume and apparently genuine jewellery, real close people, mapped on a shared terrain, whereas Napoleon was currently unmapped, it was easy to believe that, in terms of this counting-hall (and therefore of what else?), Napoleon did not count.

Does anyone without purchasing power count? Or was she talking only of invisibility, of that not intimately connected with the right-here and the right-now? Elisabet had always had trouble with this. Standing by a counter filled with small chintz hippopotami she recalled Napoleon only with a great effort of imagination, as if he lay right at the foot of that faculty's tunnel: it was almost too dark there to make him out.

But she *had* recalled him, and had received a stab not unlike physical pain, a sharp quick spasm. Then the lights seemed to flicker, to dim – for a moment she thought her inconstancy had been theatrically discovered, and that, in the next second, a critical spotlight would pick her out – people were leaving in a single-minded crowd in which she was borne. Liberty's was closing. It was 6 p.m. The benefit offices would already be shut. Or so she surmised; she had no intention of finding out. (Wasn't this, in fact, why she had squandered the whole afternoon?) Supposition, hesitating for just a second among the pouring masses of Regent's Street, thinking warmly of home, took the line of least resistance and passed itself off as fact. Yes, she said aloud, firming up the data. It was almost 6.10 now – of course they were shut. She would have to go tomorrow, that was all. And while aware that this was just another instance of that chronic procrastination which acts as a parasite on depression, Elisabet managed to shrug off her doubts. Really, to one in Napoleon's state, what difference did a day make?

Still, conscience counts. It deceives, it makes no difference to anyone but ourselves, but we sleep with it and sometimes, we think, it builds a staircase to some heaven. Therefore, in order to save the fare, which she would give to her friend, she said, and growing very cold in a wind which carried on it little bitter flecks of sleet, she began the tiresome walk, past the bus stop, past the cosy inlet to the tube, the forty-minute trudge beside Napoleon's moralising, conscience-striking ghost, all the way home to her bedsit in Victoria.

2

At present, and until something comes up, I have nothing to bestow but advice.

February 1989

At odds with the authorities on Napoleon's behalf (but, so far, fruitlessly), Elisabet felt embattled herself. Back in her room, which this afternoon seemed so independent as to be more than herself – herself as depleted by questioning and treks between hostels, none any good (Napoleon would not consider them and, though they meant to help, she could see why) – Elisabet faced another week on very short rations. The phone calls, buses and tubes had eaten heavily into her resources. What was needed, she thought, only half ironically, was a secondary subsidy enabling one to set in motion and complete the claim for the subsidy on which one had first determined – the time, effort and resources spent on these quests so seriously diminishing the few pounds obtained at the end, if they ever were, that their supportiveness was quite undermined.

It was a game much worse than snakes and

ladders. Elisabet had encountered only forfeits, only snakes lately. For instance, there were new rules now, cutting out payments for emergencies such as a jammed cistern, a burnt-out stove. Or even such routine matters as the clothes and shoes a subsistence allowance does not cover. No, the occasional help one used to get (after learning how – each area of the benefit system masquerading as a set of mysteries open only to the persistent) had been transmuted from flat payments to repayable loans, ensuring, therefore, that the borrower, without resources, must borrow again to increase his debts.

Help! In how many ways, Elisabet asked, removing her outdoor things (she had been to see a bed and breakfast place into which, it was clear, fuzzy, gentle Napoleon would not fit), can that noun and verb be interpreted? Curiously, the new system was presented as helpful – an encouragement towards independence, self-sufficiency, and that greatly prized quality, the acme of the new capitalism, self-help. Yet, as far as Napoleon and his like were concerned, one might as well be holding out a carrot to a donkey with no senses: only vivid apprehension will make that carrot, that incentive, real.

Meanwhile, isn't it a dreadful lie (she continued her thoughts lying on her bed, face to the ceiling) to pretend that, as a government, you give so much as to deserve the accolade of benefactor – a keen benefactor, tempering kindness with large doses of discipline, like some severe nanny? – when the truth is, not only do you not give as much as the voter, the constituent, would wish – but you do not give in the way that the defunct traditions of widow's mites, halved cloaks, and Buddhist non-materialism once required.

Another moral erosion she had noted was how even some of the poor are unwilling to help their fellows. You might expect more there than from remote or passing business people, but in fact the opposite can prevail. Take Napoleon's dossing-mates, the ones among whom, in the more conservative pitches, he often slept. Darien had only one interest: the £29 he got every Thursday, which went straightaway on drink. He wasn't, so Elisabet understood, a bad bloke, except for the Friday and Saturday when he was plastered, and Sunday which was painfully sobering. In his cups he was a sort of Mr Bloom, but no worse: his language was not literary, but it had colour and rhythm; it was a sort of scatalogical verse-by-the-minute, the metre marked by burpings or swigs. Somehow, a lot of laundry came into it, Elisabet had not worked out how, but she imagined that, as a young boy, he must have looked with fascination at women's washing-lines; he often mentioned garments, their right colours too, and relevant anatomy. She had a strong picture of his ideal – a large fleshy woman, a Beryl Cook, corseted in peach satin, cavernous hollows planed by her figure, brassière cups – or so she had unravelled from Darien's language – big enough for nestling, boiling whole caulis or, separately, cabbage and potato in. Perhaps he slept with his landladies?

When not drunk, Darien was amusing. Very drunk and he was offensive, and offensively sick. Napoleon's bedroll had suffered, and the first time, Napoleon had wept terribly. Then Darien, striking out with a ringed fist, had slashed a long wound down the side of his face – recalling that trauma in the Sally. But Napoleon was at least learning not to weep. More quickly than Elisabet could have imagined, he was acquiring that degree of hardness – perhaps no more than a veneer, but a resilient one – on which survival outdoors depends.

When not inebriated, Darien was a surprisingly good mate to have around, even lashing out on Napoleon's behalf if there was trouble he had not started himself. Though that was all he would do. The idea of there being anywhere to go but where he was had long ago faded: Darien was used to the non-status which two days a week he was too drunk to remember. On another level of life altogether, one which, in his cups, he could not revile too much, people slept in beds, in houses, buying food which was cooked in kitchens and eaten at tables, with clean implements. But it was as if this very simple level, the one to which Elisabet clung, took place at the top of a steep incline, a greased slope without hand or footholds, and therefore much harder than the professionals' ladder, which Darien regarded as unscalable. He had no further interest in attempting it. He was concerned only that a regular tiny proportion of the money made up there should be channelled down to provide amnesia for two nights of his week.

So Napoleon could expect neither succour nor advice from that quarter.

Mike, another neighbour, a lad with rose-blond hair and a fine skin which showed no trace of beard, seemed hardly more than a baby. Napoleon, claiming that he was nearly seventeen (he seemed younger), worried about, almost cosseted, him in the little ways still open to his kind: doubtless it made Napoleon, so unaided himself, feel stronger, slightly less unfortunate, to nurse someone whom he *imagined* less able.

Mike was another victim of the fault system, which was supposed to act as a clinical preventive (or so Elisabet believed) but took no account of personal pain. In his case, he was not entitled to receive any money, because he was under eighteen, had refused a training course, and had no address. Indeed, he could not afford an address, though when the will had been there, as it now was not, he would have been able to make himself more acceptable for daily work had he had one.

Eventually the rules would change, but Mike was not optimistic. It was his own concern why he had left home, and he wanted no one looking into that. Neither did he want to be forced on to a training course in order to do a man's work for a slave's pay. Originally, he had come to the capital full of hope: he would find a job, and somewhere to live, quick. But no opportunities had come about, and he soon saw that on the wages from unskilled work he could not afford anywhere decent to live anyway. So the street culture had claimed him and, as far as the rules were concerned – which, he predicted, would go through only a cosmetic change, because the punitive motive behind them was so strong – Mike, having chosen this cul-de-sac, was filed away, on hold until older. There was something in his babyish face, and the way he huddled his body in his torn anorak, pathetically expressive to Elisabeth of being 'on hold'. All he could do was beg or steal. Or, as she believed was often the case, scrounge from Napoleon, not only for food but for the crack which made his existence something less of a trial.

Most of Mike's friends were beggars or junkies, some clever, some abject, all very young, most well below school-leaving age:

children with old faces and a grasp of life so elderly it held no hope of anything beyond the day to day. Elisabet listened sympathetically when they told of home lives that rivalled Phillip Pirrip's, poor Pip's. Wasn't Dickens himself driven by recollected misery? She saw Fagin's new brats often enough, just less ragged but no less devious or disaffected, and at these times her spirits reached another low. Had there really been so little progress?

Looking at Napoleon with his friend, she thought that the only progress had been in the individual's ability to distance, to forget. Rare philanthropic societies apart, she thought she could honestly say, or her observations, anyway, upheld this idea, that conscience, duty, community spirit had died. From the level of the beggar, or the semi-comatose junkie/ alcoholic, London was a fast-moving stream of toe and heel, very sharp, descriptive toes and heels too, secreting just a few coppers to the mendicants on the floor as they hurried past. And no looks. No care.

She knew she was becoming like this herself. After visits to the guts and bellies of institutions bordering the river, the concrete entrails of concert halls where Napoleon sometimes hung about, one of his acquaintances having a smart wooden cabin there where he occasionally shared a bottle, or fry-up, she wanted only to forget. Luckily, Napoleon, enjoying a new kind of content with his protégé, had passed from a state of benign indignation to a lack of any kind of feeling at all about his situation. Indeed, he had almost accepted the view, quietly put forward by many who dealt with him, that his predicament was largely his own fault. He had done nothing to help himself, wasn't this true? Wasn't *his own apathy* the reason why (official voices slowing at this point, in order to spell it out) all efforts to 'help him' had failed. And why (although they used every euphemism to give the case a more seemly construction), in Elisabet's words, he was a reject: a homeless, dirty, odorous, and therefore increasingly unwanted – surplus – man.

Of course, it all came down not to the beginnings but to Napoleon. Elisabet saw this view – the official view – like an automatic emission of fumes or excreta: to pass on blame keeps a system feeling healthy, and although she did not know which body was at fault, she rather believed that the great and clumsy socially intervening apparatus (social as in DSS), which, politics apart, must be placentally, fiscally, linked to government, was not as caring as it believed.

From her standpoint, it seemed to *care* only where it could *do* – that is, where abilities (its) and need (the client's) met and found common purpose. It was rather like laying a paper pattern over a piece of material: cut where marked. Whole areas, not yet officially recognised, or no longer catered for, are not touched. She had seen the same thing happen with near-lunatics, for whom there was no longer provision (neither homes, nor institutions, nor effective drugs) and therefore no kind of help.

Sadly, even where they felt most capable, where there were sparks of hope (yes, this problem could be 'managed'), she found the administrators tired, indifferent – not so far removed from the hopelessness which should distinguish their clients.

If this was the case, how could they, fatigued by burgeoning problems which were, luckily, not their own, blame poor Napoleon, who had been exhausted from birth? Prescience was there at the start, waiting for him by the cradle: his childhood had been poor as a stony, overtilled field and things had never improved. As if taking on board without question his life's lack of promise, the young Napoleon had dragged himself wearily from watershed to watershed, without hope. She thought that this inherent lethargy, together with prolonged immaturity and naïveté, facts of character being steadily preserved by hardship, like any anomaly within resin, were the only faults that could be justly laid at his door. Though she did wonder, staring at the new shape of shadow on her ceiling, for how long he would remain naïve about Mike.

Sharing with Mike, he had barely enough to feed himself. It was stupid. Yet even Elisabet felt her heart hardening, as it must within the shirts, blouses, T-shirts, city waistcoats of all those passing by Napoleon and his kind, throwing nothing, or so little it amounted to nothing, into the begging bowls they offered; as it must within the sleek garments of the men and women who created the legislation of which Mike had fallen foul and which discriminated, too, against poor Napoleon. To remain solvent, which is the beginning of solid prosperity, one needs a heart like a rock. Elisabet had just over £100 in the building society, savings which, so far, had stood between herself and abjectness, savings into which she had dipped for a tiny amount, almost every week when not working, because she could not make what money she received stretch – latterly she had had even less money, because someone had seen fit, for reasons she could not understand (they had not been given), to cut her benefit. If she dipped into these savings on Napoleon's behalf also, they would disappear faster, she would reach the absolute brink sooner. What would Elisabet do then? They would disappear anyway, she knew that, but, as Wilkins Micawber would agree, no need to cry yet, because there, like a pillow under the head, or an old coat reasonably defensive against cold, they still were.

Why, oh why, couldn't Napoleon – those thin dirty fingers, she felt, as she lay in her room, plucking at her resources – why couldn't Napoleon help himself?

Elisabet sighed and got up from the bed. She was being awfully unjust. She would be better employed making a cup of tea – this was about the limit of her own self-aid. Look how she could not persuade anyone to give her more money; the converse had occurred. And how she could not secure decent employment, though she was still supposed to go through the motions of trying to. It was even said that, shortly, evidence of these efforts would be needed; she must provide documentation, although this would be difficult. Elisabet had long passed the stage of formally applying for jobs. She had been in the habit latterly of asking at counters, or at shops and cafés where they posted 'Wanted' cards, and where, if she met an oblique refusal, there was never any proof. The sharp young woman at the Jobcentre did not believe her; nor did she believe Elisabet when she said she was 'frightened' of the rows of identical, wipe-clean cards which rapped out details and salaries of jobs with expectations of staying power she knew she could not meet; and requirements regarding interviews which she knew would hurt and probably crush.

But just to make sure she would not lose out (because, as they said, by law she was required to do this, and she knew the forfeit system too well to quibble), she began presenting herself at an agency dealing with casual labour – clerks, typists, that sort of thing; or at a shop requiring assistants; or a catering firm needing waitresses. And was sometimes taken on for a day or two. Never more. She wasn't sure why. It might have something to do with her clothes, replacing which was out of the question. Years old and unfashionable, they and Elisabet had accommodated themselves to each other; they suited her better than the frumpy, stale-smelling garments in charity shops – all she could run to if she dipped into the £100. And quite unaffordable on the subsistence allowance, which, as she had pointed out to many impervious administrators, feeds but does not otherwise succour.

Or were employers put off by her face? And that mark of absence which glances in shop windows discovered as a sort of stigma or even, more ineradicably, physical blemish? A cast more sinister than the mere dreaminess she was accused of in childhood, it was nevertheless a true mirror, as true as if the face, centuries ago, had learnt techniques only latterly available to medicine: she meant with the swift and painfully descriptive speculum, or the laparoscope, all those –scopes. For it was true, as her features claimed, that her mind, and the seat of her emotions, wherever that could be, were in a continual soup these days. She had difficulty in attending: was absent-minded, she forgot or muddled a customer's order or change. She thought it was not serious, not a pathological problem, like Napoleon's, but an apathy instigated by depression.

She no longer had any interest in being bright. Numbness had invaded, blocking the mind's sharp, interconnecting corridors, and her thoughts, which she had once thought of as quick, fairly intelligent little mice, scuttling usefully, self-improvingly round an elastic cranial network – and necessarily mating, begetting – were now dull-furred, anaemic, lethargic. Mostly, for want of sustenance and encouragement, they slept at the end of dusty cul-de-sacs. Only the subject of money aroused a quiver; it touched their nostrils with spicy breath. Poor mice. She could not blame them. What was there, apart from the above, to stimulate or worry about?

Studying herself after each rejection or very short-term job, Elisabet tried to look less abstract. Or to take the extreme view, less daft. And although she *could* remodel her face, especially by smiling, she could not change the expression of her eyes. A jaundiced glaze sat over their blueness; the lids drooped more than they used to. There was a lack of sharpness which, at her best, made her look like someone who has just been shocked by a bad accident. At her worst . . . well.

Another point Elisabet noticed is how poverty makes people ugly. This applied to herself. She thought she had been pretty once – was almost sure she had. But a kind of discoloration, similar to that of malnutrition, had appeared, while the shape of her face had changed. Where, for instance, was her chin? It had fallen into the shallow pouch scalloped from jaw to neck. Something also had happened to her circulation. She could no longer raise any pinkness from the base film which earlier, on Napoleon, she had thought to be dirt.

Diet apart (hers was as good as she could afford), she was convinced now that feelings have colour, settling, as auras do, over and around the outer membrane before infiltrating hair, skin, etc. like the slow, self-propagating flame of some conspiracy versus nature. The poor, the minerally debased, cannot shine as the well-fed and unworried, especially as the wealthy, sleekly do.

The inescapable fact was that you looked as you felt, not the other way round, as beauticians, with a vested interest, would have it. Each time

Elisabet glimpsed her tense image her small spirits plummeted, for it was clear that she had slipped through the nets of femininity and was only a hard-luck case. In her particular echelon, close by the echelons of the city's refugees, nervously encamped in proximity to their own urine wherever they were allowed, sex's best value – and surely Elisabet would do well to remember this – was as a commodity, a transaction whose price is a dinner, drugs or dress. She wanted to say yes, but wait (said it to her intemperate kettle, which always spilled water when it boiled), in Napoleon's group there are also lovers. But when she saw their youth and simplicity she thought of puppies. In other areas she had witnessed the reflex habit which was not *so* different to corner copulation, dogs.

Dreary thoughts. She would not, then, as she carried her cup of tea to the chair by the window, consult the pear-wood mirror, an old friend to whom she regularly said hello. It was not needed for a simple reknotting of hair, accomplished quickly, standing against the curtain. No luxuries, such as hairdressers – who are sent, ironically, to hospitals to perk up the dying. If prospective employers did not like her looks, that was too bad. Since major alterations are in the luxury class, there was not a thing, not an adjective or an area, that such handfuls of small change as she had could improve. 'Poor

women, like pieces of cheap design,' Elisabet
said to the air, 'must therefore remain as they are
– disfigured by status.'

She had not, however, finished with her
friend's cause, although this evening she was
ready to recognise that shut-off, don't-want-to-
care attitude which signals defeat. It had for
some time now characterised Nap. He was, he
looked, awfully tired. His head, he had said once,
literally holding it, hurt from all the questions. It
felt battered because, for him, metaphors were
real, and the general response to his pleas a hard
stone wall. She noticed how quickly, as if to
concede defeat, and wisely expecting nothing
from Elisabet's skirmishes, he had changed in his
month or so on the street. He had become
thinner and paler beneath his discoloration;
there was a disconcerting edge to his passivity, a
hardness or callous beyond that necessary for
self-defence. Not that he didn't need it, a shell,
the days being sometimes as bad as the nights.
Harassment in broad daylight, yes.

Looking out of the window, Elisabet sipped
her tea and wondered if, when the time came, as
she was sure it would, she could make herself
similar equipment with which to ward off theft,
abuse, rape, the unruliness which, as Napoleon
wailed, often broke out. But when, hearing a
neighbour's radio snap on, and the constant blare
of sport invade her room – when, with her cup

against her chest, she looked inside herself for resources, she found only, pressed behind her eyelids, the inevitable self-pitying well of tears.

What would Mother have thought? And Father? Stupid questions, they arose, she believed, so as to show up the full extent of her abasement. Mother and Father, especially as she always pictured them, neat, well tailored, with a house effortlessly run with cheap 'help', Mother sewing in mid-afternoon among the hideously plumped, dull Dralons of the drawing-room, Father, on Sundays, paying bills at the oak dropleaf which had come down from his mother – the personages of these images towered in her mind with the indignation of patriarchs, livid, on the mountain side, indicting tablets in their hands, the excesses of their people displayed in colourful encampment below; her parents' figures, stiff with affront, an angry flush crimsoning their faces stood, as a stained-glass panel might, against the sun streaming dustily through her window. Somehow, Father had got her building society book in his hand.

'£117.36. Is this *all* you have left, Elisabet?'

'Surely, dear, there's some mistake?' Mother's voice, when most disbelieving, was most soft, as butter might be, melting round a hard-bladed knife.

'But you received the shares, didn't you? So

kind of Uncle Graham. And a jolly good investment, Elisabet. Tin.'

(Yes, £1,300 odd. Then.)

'Oh, and Elisabet, look at your *hair*. What
have you done to it . . . And goodness. Is this
where you *live*?'

'Elisabet, you do have a job, don't you?' (That
tone, ideal for a hell-fire preacher. Or sadist,
head teacher . . .)

'Surely . . .'

'Elisabet . . .'

'Mr Micawber's difficulties are almost overwhelming just at present,' said Mrs Micawber ... 'When I lived at home with papa and mama, I really should have hardly understood what the word meant, in the sense in which I now employ it, but experientia does it* – as papa used to say.'

1955–1960

Oh, but she could run through it all in five minutes – how each little bit of money she had ever had had quickly amounted to nothing. Only the small windfall from Uncle Graham survived, the bulk much depleted, and not only because she had, luckily, traded the shares before the slump but because here, alone, Elisabet had been severe with herself. *Don't touch!* had become a maxim which, though not followed to the letter, kept her inroads down to the level of petty pilfering. An achievement, given the frequency of her depressions and their counter-command: *Spend!* But her sole achievement, and not much to her credit, since it was only savings.

*A play on *experientia docet* – experience teaches

The trouble was that Elisabet at eighteen, though not lacking in ability, had not been forward-thinking. There had been nothing wrong with her education, nor her teachers' exhortations: she counted a civil engineer, secondary headmistress, obstetric surgeon, two journalists (technical and tabloid) and a moderately famous actress among her classmates. But they were rather different girls, their ambitions evident so early that puberty seemed hardly to touch them.

They were neat, organised, forward-thinking, always properly equipped (set squares for trig, overalls for art, wellies for the fieldwork announced last week), had done their homework, left nothing vital at home, knew where and what the next lesson was. They were 'self-starters', as someone in the eighties belatedly put it.

Crumpled and haphazard, Elisabet spent her school career watching a bee trapped in the classroom window, or reading under her desk lid, no matter how many times she was caught, the bad, weepy novels which created something close to a minefield in her quarterly report. When not bored, even in literature classes, when she yawned over *Cranford* and Auden, she was usually in love, in love with everyone. That was why she sat by the classroom window, so that she could fall in love with the young men come to renovate the boiler; with the builders adding the extension (two classrooms and a gym); with the

47

youths who hung around the school gates in order to leer at plaited, newly voluptuous adolescents on their way to buy ice creams, or pomegranates, whose seeds they picked off with pins, smacking purpled mouths on the way back from the shop. She was no prettier than her friends, but her hair being longer, blonder, and arranged so as to bounce on her knitted bust, she liked to think the youths leered particularly at her, or at that part of her anatomy the gym mistress surely meant when, not looking down there, she whispered: 'You have nicely developed – calves, Elisabet.'

Then she had fallen in love with the Music master and the English master and, more in the Austen tradition, with the new curate at church, and the young Roman priest who gave the school papists communion every Friday. In short, she had fallen in love with every eligible male who came within her sphere of experience. She fell in love also, copiously, with characters in books and large, smooth, black-and-white film stars. For years she had a passion for Olivier, always ready to step up and fill the place in his life left so dramatically vacant by Vivien Leigh.

Existence was therefore so coloured and peopled she had little time for school, where, it seemed, life had been reduced to a hard, dry biscuit, or packet of biscuits. 'But, Elisabet, don't you see the *beauty* of Latin?' Cornered during a detention imposed for not learning irregular verbs, Elisabet boldly replied that, yes, she saw the beauty of it, but the beauty was an abstract thing, like a painting by Raoul Dufy, or a vase by Lucy Rie: she felt obliged to appreciate from the outside an artefact whose finer qualities (so Art Appreciation taught) she did not understand and had no desire to emulate.

Elisabet got away with a lecture, to which she half listened – this was enough for teachers, who talked automatically, like radios – while watching the heating-apprentice across the yard. She never did learn those verbs, though she greatly admired the syncopation of different tenses, with their final clusters of alternating vowels ranked, like small bands of Roman legionaries, some fleshier, some sparer, across the page.

Neither did she escape as quickly as she hoped. She was in for seven years, all transparent escapist ruses, like all attempts to win her interest, having failed. Only once was imagination captured: that morning when a bright young married woman breezed into the classroom, quite unannounced, and began talking for a whole hour about – the girls could hardly believe it – the physical side of marriage, making explicit references to her husband, his parts, and what seemed, though there was an aspect to it almost like engineering, a very chummy partnership.

The point was contraception. Someone in the hierarchy had correctly sized up the girls, who were keen to learn what Biology had skated over – not only the engineering, but the different kinds of tool you could apply, and where, and how, in order to derive maximum enjoyment without the nuisance of babies. The couple had tried almost everything and were still triumphantly childless. Elisabet, craning eagerly forward, particularly admired the lustre in the young woman's eyes and the pink highlights, almost as if painted in, on her cheeks. She appeared to hold within herself a shining, quivering key to something none of their spinster teachers had. It was easy to see what it was, but not easy to understand how it had escaped their married mistresses. Yet escape it had, because there was no visible difference between settled and single teachers (frizzled perms, liverish eyes, air of overstretched patience) unless you looked, as one looked at tickets in cattle markets or on shop shelves, for the band which had dug itself in, third finger, left hand. No shimmer, no difference. How could this be?

Like most of the girls looking forward to the end of seven years' internment, Elisabet resolved to find out. Mr and Mrs Stern, however, had other plans. Hardly had leaving day come when, exasperated but undefeated, they packed the girl off to a funny narrow building close to Harrods which claimed to do something in the way of 'finishing'. Here a certain sloppiness was removed from her speech, while her vowels were tucked and pinched, her consonants ironed. To please them she learnt to speak with an only partly opened mouth, drawing her lips well back, somewhat like an oyster opening and closing its shell, as the advice of disdainful hairdressers and clinical beauticians was sought; while she was pummelled and punched, rollered and lacquered until she emerged looking not at all like herself. It was disconcerting to become more of a product than a person, but she didn't really mind. The lectures about flower-arranging, pastry-making and what you might call shopper's French, the lessons, yes, about shopping, were much more comfortable if you felt, as she looked, a complete imposter.

After the light, not desperately boring classes of the morning, they went upstairs to rooms which were airless even with windows cranked to their limits to learn the spidery codes of shorthand and skills for mastering ancient manual typewriters. Privately, Elisabet referred to the activity as 'riding', because their machines, harnessed with ribbon, oiled and over exercised, with certain constructions like bits and stirrups had, like all commercial ponies, mean, stubborn minds of their own. And each typewriter, like each horse, as you will know if you have ever been riding, has a separate mind of its own, not inclined to recognise skills which, mounted, one was obliged to display: guidance, walking, trotting, cantering, dressage – and the mastery which is both the sum and the binding theory of these parts.

It was a matter of proceeding with caution (only that, the teachers said) and getting to know your mount. Beginners who galloped fell off, with their keys in a horrible jam and the ribbon mashed in the bit, while a nice piece of dressage was a difficult letter done without effort – indentation, tabulation, headings, subheadings, numbered points – all a matter of course, a smooth excursion for swots with adroit fingers and rock-steady wrists.

But Elisabet was Elisabet, scarcely listening to a word her teachers said. She set off at a canter the moment she could and fell with an awful wrenching screech from her machine, catching a nasty bruise from the carriage. Shorthand went no better. Her mind stalled at rigours which depend not on large, bold, expressive stabs, and a page of arrant nonsense, but on practice, memory, practice, memory, *finesse*.

Still, she had eighteen months.

'You understand, don't you, Elisabet, that you are going to get a job at the end of all this. I do *not* intend to keep you. Good God, you've cost enough as it is.' Father spoke frequently in this manner, back to the fire, which he thus kept from Elisabet, who, squashed into a corner of the sofa, was forced to focus on his buttoned-tweed flies, the source of much impertinent speculation. They had never satisfactorily explained why she was an only child.

She knew what they intended. This had been the point of the finishing institution, to occupy and further groom her until she married, transferring what had become just a liability to another man's bank balance and management. But she did not mind too much, not yet. All these arrangements required little of her apart from attendance. Beyond their formal acts, somehow merging into their nuisance, though she did not yet see how, stretched independence, men, the future.

If. If is the logarithm from which the past's value may be calculated. Some happy futures never require it: their tables of 'ifs' are locked in a drawer, unused. The connections were good, the calculations easy and accurate, one point leading to another without equivocation. The future, when it arrived, needed no further analysis. On the other hand, some people's tables are dog-eared, their covers missing, a heavy use obvious. Look carefully at the abstracted face of an unhappy man or woman and you can be sure of what they are thumbing through. *If* is the grid marrying event and result. *If* is simple: it supplies the reason why, or why not.

For instance, if only Elisabet could have chosen where to work. If only she had had the resources to leave home earlier, avoiding what happened at O'Malley's. But Father moved swiftly, arranging a position to start the very Monday after finishing at the institution close to Harrods. *If only*. Florid, plump, twenty years too old and not the least bit sexy, O'Malley would hardly have figured as a choice. He was a solicitor, like Father, and a member of the Lodge. Elisabet could only imagine what had passed between, what promises on both sides had been made. One thing was certain: O'Malley would have been sworn to patience, perhaps for some paltry Masonic return, patience and per-severance while 'the problem', as Mother called her, settled down to find her feet.

What feet? If her parents meant financial and social ones, Elisabet had other ideas. While at the typewriter, her salaried appendages slipped easily from their stirrups: the machine ran away even when she thought she had control, her letters being rich with anagrams, her legal documents a sort of artwork of carbon thumbs and rubbings-out so vicious that superimpositions would not take. To get them, as was required, mistake-free, she was forced to hobble, clatter-bang-clatter, at a punitive rate.

'You are costing me,' O'Malley would pretend to joke, coming close to eye her hips or calves, while he glanced casually at the work in her machine. Sometimes he would creep up behind and stare down the V-neck of her blouse, spiritous breath quickening. She could almost hear his heart race, but what could she do? Cover herself? The crisp, plunging collar was standard office wear; no one with any nous wore them round.

Crocket, senior secretary, pretended not to notice. She had weighed Elisabet up; she had made an experienced notation. They spoke only in the mornings, or the evenings, or about botched tasks, or the tea which Elisabet was always so late in producing. Each remark was a masterpiece of minimalism: Elisabet had not known before that so much meaning could pack so short a space. Her 'Good night, Miss Stern' was the neatest, accompanied by a shrewd look at Elisabet's desperate key-bashing and the full waste-paper bin between her knees.

Somehow, Elisabet got worse rather than better. Her late evenings grew later and later as she struggled to complete tasks until, through fatigue and desperation for a better slice of leisure, she succumbed to the way of managing O'Malley that O'Malley wanted.

Funny how, to think back on it, that period was

as sinister as it was comic. Sometimes Elisabet enjoyed the comedy. At other times it was the menacing overtones she enjoyed. There was something Hitchcockian about the distortions – warped furniture, ballooning shadows, top-lit, bent, foreshortened heads – in the starkly illuminated back office where, on those early winter evenings, under the single too-powerful bulb, Crocket hurried to complete her suddenly doubled workload while Elisabet typed slower and slower in order to legitimise her lingering in the office. For the first time Elisabet enjoyed secret sexual knowledge as she watched out for beads of moisture on Crocket's brow, or the smiles of duplicity sent her way when O'Malley, carrying documents, crossed behind Miss Crocket's back. As 5.30 neared she would become aware of O'Malley's restlessness behind the part-glazed door as he crossed, recrossed his room, rattled the filing cabinet, lifted, dropped the telephone, coughed, agitated his swivel chair, strained, like herself, for signs that Miss Crocket was at last covering her typewriter, sweeping the post ostentatiously into her bag, clearing up her things.

The tension between them was so strong they could have been plotting a murder. Yet it was innocent, it was only a game as far as Elisabet was concerned, and for a while they observed the rules, O'Malley calling for her, with shorthand book, just before or just after Miss Crocket's aggrieved departure. It would not do for Elisabet to be always, at that point, already installed in the inner office, engaged in the game that O'Malley, without so much as a word, and with complete disregard for his promises to Father, had indicated as an option from the very day she took the job.

Looks was all it came to at first, and looks Elisabet did not much mind, for life, which had stymied, must be urged on, and this was experience – a sort of parade for O'Malley's benefit: the shortened skirt exposing a firm, kittenishly waving calf, the plump crossed knee, even an inch or so of thigh. She grew adept at unbuttoning and buttoning up the top of her blouse on the threshold of his room, and tossing back hair and head to show a throat whose major attraction, for O'Malley, her mirror was not precise about.

In fact it was through O'Malley's eyes that she came to understand, just as if she were some artwork set out for public approval, what her exterior surface, through parts and arrangement to final gloss, must mean. Mirrors, with their subjective returns and reversals, are not satisfactory for the exacting. Up to now Elisabet had been certain only that she was not ugly and not entirely contemporary; beyond that categorisation eluded. What was needed – she learnt, of course, when she got it – was the commentary O'Malley supplied as his eye looked, roved, moulded, clarified, from the first, his exegetical attitude. And there Elisabet – only much later asking herself if he might have been as wrong as he was biased – looking at her image in the keen surface of his lust, discovered what, in this sphere, she was.

Funnily, the end product was not as clear, or like a painting, as she might have hoped. It was more of an opaque sculpture, a marvel of shape polished up by masculine eyes, but quite indifferent to inner workings.

Never mind. It was only looking. Or was until, one late afternoon, during their sham dictation, which he took at the pace of ordinary speech, and just after the slam of the door behind Crocket, he reached out a hot hand and touched her knee where it lay shinily engorged across the other. More. Having touched, he began to squeeze, gradually contracting the muscles until the flesh reddened and hurt. She looked at the hand, fascinated, until it relaxed and began a rhythmic massage. It even began to move – up. She knew she must make a decision.

So it hadn't been only flirtation after all. She had been wrong about his side of it, and now there was this, her first critical decision. Should she? Or shouldn't she? There was no doubt about what O'Malley intended. Giving in, going along

with him, would be easiest. It represented the
essential experience, and once such a bad
scholar, she was awfully impatient to learn, the
image of the flushed young wife, lecturing on
contraception, still teased – though somehow she
did not see O'Malley supplying the enviable
afterglow, did not see her fulfilment dependent
on his fleshy lips, his inflamed breath, his
paunch . . .

Not first choice, then. But . . . the older man, a
man of not inconsiderable means, never mind for
the moment that the means were supplied by his
wife, suggested certain advantages, or should we
say *gifts*, which had already been imaginatively
catalogued – they were her only antidote to
boredom and typist's cramp. Of course, they
would take a little *time* to acquire: a suite in a top,
better than local hotel; use of – ownership of, the
imagination does run – a chauffeured Bentley;
ample wardrobe of fur-trimmed 'at homes' and
scooped-neck satin dresses; bouncy, impregnable
Monroe perm – a fascinating catalogue, whose
logistics did not concern her. The goods would
come, she said, almost with a flick of the wrist, a
smooth, flawless, priceless wrist, they would
arrive, she was worth it, worth the whole lot,
should she ever . . .

However. There were, from this point of
view, at very close proximity to O'Malley, a
great many 'howevers' about it. If put to it, for

instance, she would have to say that he did not look, or smell, like the kind of man to furnish such dreams. While, if you were thinking of bargaining, of getting the first credit on that imaginary shopping list, it was not herself who, at the moment, had the advantage. (She moved her leg a little, to stall him, but the massaging and creeping upwards continued even as O'Malley's dictating voice droned on.)

Yes, the big problem was that not only had she been surprised but that in this state of surprise there was no time to count and consider all the 'howevers' and 'ifs', because this type of thinking is very laborious if done properly, requiring a different time scale from that of an eager hand moving anticipatorily up a leg. The two don't synchronise. There was, in fact, barely a moment to glance at the consequences both of acceptance and refusal – though she felt, felt rather rapidly and hotly, that 'No' and a firm pushing back of his fingers would lead directly to her resignation. She could not see herself coming in, as normal, the day after, having done that, just as she could not see O'Malley, so grandly, swallowing so much pride.

But suddenly the time for debate ran out. This was always to be the trick with her critical decisions – Elisabet never had enough of the right kind of time, and when she had it, she was going to employ it all wrongly, never believing in the long periods required for judicious thought, or that courses may be altered quite slowly. She would put off everything to the last moment and then be panicked, just as always, as now in the moment before extremity, or on the night before exams.

If this was a test, then she had failed it, failed it at the point of juggling between furs and postponement for a handsomer, more endearing sort of man; failed miserably, for O'Malley's hand, dithering deceptively over the stocking-top, speeded up the last six inches and, in the second instance of things happening through non-intervention, claimed its goal. Her goose, then, was cooked.

In every way the incident was prophetic. What she felt, both as person and body, was to be repeated, in ways varying in pleasantness, until, somewhere in her forties, she decided that the pleasure had gone for good and she found the process at best funny, at worst distasteful, while what she now saw, as she endured with eyes sealed (apart from the odd curious peek) was that she was very inadequately prepared: one might say, with all due deference to the contraceptive lady, totally unprepared. It was just no good to be dim about anatomy and trust to luck. *He* knew; but that Elisabet did not did not help. On the contrary. While it occurred to her towards the end that, if she had known, known exactly what it came down to – she realised now what a cosmetic veil the contraceptive lady had thrown – she wouldn't have. Or not with O'Malley.

As it was, she did, uncomfortably perched on his desk, her clothes bundled about her person (she did not look at her assailant, but she heard his trousers, with their pockets full of heavy change, drop), her skin shrinking where his hands seemed to take on eyes, ogling rather than fondling. In fact, O'Malley was ghastly: lewd, lecherous – so *embarrassing*. His wet, warm mouth sucked and probed (she knew it was his mouth because of the hot whiskyish breath that came with it; yes, he had tippled himself up to it) and his hands were as clumsy as his other part, their only virtue, if you could call it that, was that all three knew exactly where to go.

Strangely enough, O'Malley was not at all embarrassed – which made her wonder what his wife and the others (lots of women, they said; O'Malley wasn't choosy) had to endure. Did he really think that he was skilled, that he had *seduced* her?

Wilful disbelief. This is how Elisabet later came to classify an attitude she met time and again, met in about half of the men she had sex with, went to bed with (though perhaps this was not a bad average?). The doing was all. After, it was only Elisabet, coping with a failure not all her failure, sometimes not any of it *her* failure, she believed – who did any analysis. As things went, and went on, she grew certain of that.

But back to the wintry afternoon. It was done. As at so many points yet to come, that was all that could be said for it. Elisabet was filled with regret. She was too angry to cry, and too sore; besides, blubbing indicated a weakness which, perish the thought, might inspire O'Malley to have another try. He was still game; he would not let her go, though puffing and beginning to hiccup, until she broke free and, gathering her garments in a sort of cummerbund round her body, luckly finding her shoes, made off, with the briefest explanation, for the lavatory, not even nodding when he gasped something inaudible, in a tone of voice which redoubled her resolve not, not ever, to go back.

Impulse is a mistake if you want references and a career. Elisabet was to find this confirmed again and again. As far as O'Malley was concerned, she found she was in more of a pickle than she had first thought. For she had not said no; she had said, or indicated, yes. Then she had put such a derogatory comment on that 'Yes' that she would have been better declining in the first place, and calmly working out her resignation. No such option now. How long had O'Malley waited for her to return from the lavatory? What had been his mood when finally he himself had left? She could not imagine, any more than she could imagine facing him the very next morning.

It was indisputable, then, as several days of calmer reflection confirmed. She could not go back.

'What? Leave O'Malley and Harkness?' On these occasions, Father and Mother were interchangeable. 'You've only been there *six months*.'

At first, there'd been an easy excuse about a cold, with which circumstances, or symptoms, conspired. Agitation made her alternately flushed and white, while whenever Mother approached with a thermometer she could raise a temperature just by thinking of O'Malley. Or wondering if, by some misfortune, he'd got her in the club. Luckily, this particular question cleared itself during the dragging but necessary week in bed. The next weekend passed, and Elisabet, lonely in a house which worked more like a machine than a home, exhausted by the prim expectations of parents which seemed to hang, like old clothes, in dust covers along all the passages, from the picture rails, in every aseptic corner, recovered her metal.

'What? Leave O'Malley and Harkness?'

Dust was hardly the word for what came out of the final confrontation, Elisabet considering it her duty to stand and be slandered while she tried to explain. Perhaps she could have left a note on her pillow after all? For it was even worse than expected, if you considered not the venom but the honesty with which her parents seemed to speak. Elisabet was called by almost every name, and threatened with almost everything, including excision from Father's will. But she did not flinch, holding herself stoutly, like a warrior shouldering a sword, a sort of crusader for freedom and justice and independence. What they said did not harm her so much as their horrible blindness to her needs. It was the attitude, the intransigence, which wounded.

Anyway, Father would not die for ages – she told him as much. All their threats were idle, they could not harm her, for she was leaving. She did not give a toss for their possessions, for their dignity, for their views. Not, as she said more than once, one bloody toss.

Elisabet was not entirely wrong about O'Malley. In the end he was sharp enough to supply a terse reference and pay up to the end of that week. The three-line letter had been dictated in shame and typed with relish. There was a precision about it which amounted almost to malice. The extraordinary, super-ordinary crispness, for instance, as if Crocket had specially filed and polished the typeface of her machine; the exact positioning, into equal margins, of the fresh second-class stamp; and the complete omission of Elisabet's Christian name, as if it had never been used among them, while, as a finishing-touch, the dubious area where she roomed had been underlined in double-typed black, so heavily applied it had almost incised the envelope. Earl's Court. Elisabet could almost hear Crocket murmuring as she ripped the envelope from the platen: 'Disgusting. Full of coloureds. But not, if I may say so, surprising.'

Personally, Elisabet loved the name with its debased ring, loved everything about the dirty, seedy, crowded, cosmopolitan area. The drawback was, job-finding took longer than imagined, London being, as she had not anticipated, as full of work as of choosy and reluctant employers, and dubious and uninviting jobs. In the end she took a post with a milliner who looked at her, looked at her barely satisfactory therefore unsatisfactory reference, and, having studied both again, put her to work in the back office, where she looked down over the balustrade at incoming customers. She was not nearly as ravishing as the smooth young acolyte who sold the hats and modelled them sometimes, but her voluptuousness proved useful. The men, while waiting for girlfriends or wives, would be drawn to Elisabet's level: it was just up three linoleumed stairs. Did they too want to look down the V-neck of her blouse? She was surprised at the number of assignations she was offered, and sometimes accepted, while Margot, in the front, who wore more and better pearls against cashmeres as silky and insubstantial as dandelion clocks, sold only, as far as she could tell, hats.

Elisabet's typing did not improve, while her shorthand refused to be resurrected from the torpor into which it had sunk at O'Malley and Harkness. She muddled along, and was eventually surprised to find she had been muddling along for years, drifting around the retail trade, graduating, by way of ladies' fashions, to furs, and moving back, through lingerie, to hats. On the whole she preferred hats, whose stocktakings and pickings were easy.

Her sex life muddled along too. Though there was no real love on either side, she, they – mostly men picked up at the shop – enjoyed relationships of the cosy, furtive, fleshy sort. To her bewilderment, the straying husbands and boyfriends sometimes left money, crumpled notes on the bedside table. This hurt, but she did not refuse. The going was difficult; she could only just afford her bedsit and food, with the occasional odd night at the pictures, sometimes a tea dance or hop.

There did not seem to be time or opportunity to meet the right kind of man. No one of that sort approached, though she felt that she was not, at least, turning into an ignorant prude. On the contrary, she was acquiring extensive experience, wonderful vicarious experience, which was bound to be of use with – Prince Charming? Soon her men friends began saying, with a great deal of appreciation and fond touches, that, actually, she was awfully good in bed. Awfully inventive and responsive. Awfully *warm*. (Yes, Elisabet commented to herself. You see, I analyse, reflect. And I'm lonely too . . .) Whereas poor Sally or Judith or Delia was . . .

And then it was the sixties.

4

'The luxuries of the old country,' said Mr Micawber, with an intense satisfaction in their renouncement, 'we abandon. The denizens of the forest cannot, of course, expect to participate in the refinements of the land of the Free.'

1965–1988

To be exact it was 1965 when Elisabet woke up. Millinery was less popular. Fashion was changing dramatically, decreeing that girls like Elisabet were too plump for minis, deficiency emphasising the awkward stage she was at, on the verge of thirty and, when she studied herself closely, not only fat-legged but soiled. Yes, she looked soiled – it was the only word for it. Used, stained and thrown aside, an uncontemporary artefact. London was buzzing with young women of sharply modern feature and figure and appallingly low ages, playing loud music above her head in the lodging houses through which she was moving rapidly, because in each, like an elderly but not unenlightened spinster, she now felt out of place. The men she passed on the stairs grew younger or, at the other end of the scale, were older and ostentatiously, Elisabet's mother would say tastelessly, monied. They never seemed to see Elisabet as she paused to let them pass, only the long, young legs in short skirts they were breathlessly following after.

Not that these changes were sudden. Only that, for a while, she had been able to blinker herself from them, never having the gift of distinguishing between trends that will last, becoming solid conduits of transition, and those that die in a day. She was blinkered, to her cost, for a period unable to believe that the increased supply of money was finding its way into younger and younger hands, while she herself seemed to have less and less. Ergo, when the hat shop she was working for closed – girls now bought something cheap and dispensable from Quant or C & A – she became, for the first time, unemployed. Then she found work, and lost work. The pattern began which was to continue for twenty-odd years, with a steady downward drift, as the positions became less and less salubrious and Elisabet's skills, like her confidence, eroded.

What employers forgive in a girl who is nineteen, or twentyish, disenchants in a woman of thirty and something. Soon close on thirty-five, Elisabet began falling financially behind, evading her landlord and accruing other debts, while, simultaneously, as if they had sniffed her out, friends grew cold and distant. They were married to clever husbands, or single, on the make themselves, seizing opportunities and, alongside, as casually, as if they were merely removing unwanted accessories – an old scarf, pair of gloves, some boots – sharpening up their circles of friends.

Things were moving fast. History, you might say, had been seized and accelerated by the young. It was driven around with great noise and pomp, like the latest Harley Davidson. Elisabet, who was not asked to join in, felt there must be something noxious about her, unpleasant as an odour or skin disease with which they feared contact. She was only a little plump and not flashily employed, but she could not keep up, the gulf between herself and what seemed to be the rest, the on-going party, widening and widening until, in just two years, the names in her address book had halved, quartered, finally condensed to an inaccurate smattering.

For the first time she began to wonder about poverty.

'Oh really, Lizzie, can't you do something about yourself?'

Sometimes she went home, where it was warm and clean, the food ample if dull. Father and Mother, in their sixties now, could not, if only for gossip's sake, maintain distance. To have some news of an only daughter was better than none, while Elisabet tried to mitigate the pain her presence caused by being tidy, bright and telling lies, sometimes very quick and inventive lies, for a long-standing fiction had her as secretary in a large retail outfit, her address a shared house in Ealing. But the latter was only the marital home of a dull but obliging friend.

Or at least, Father and Mother gave lip service to the fiction. This was all that was required. Poor Eleanor, Elisabet's mother, could not help many sly, sideways looks and a momentary flinching whenever Elisabet entered the room, as if she was a dog with a bad smell, just as she seemed to restrain herself from following in her steps with air-freshener and a damp rag. Father, spine faithful to wartime service, kissed her cheek with pained surprise, and when forced to converse addressed a point beyond her left shoulder, as if there was someone there in urgent need of advice. Mostly, they met only at meal-times, those skirmishes which, in divided families, take on the urgency, if not the full penalties, of a military exercise.

But the visits were worth it, in that Mother always slipped across a cheque or notes as she was leaving. Possibly as a result of fatigue, Elisabet no longer felt amused or bitter; she was angry that she didn't but, on the contrary, found she was beginning to look at herself through their eyes and be – wasn't it true? – *apologetic*. Beside a neat, decorous mother, who smelt of powder and Yardley's creams, and Father, with his extreme fortitude, among their immaculate furniture, in the acerbic light from thoroughly Windowlened windows, where her room was kept intact, as if they had already lost their only child, Elisabet felt tarnished, soiled – extraneous.

Somewhere towards the end of the sixties her face lost the last vestige of that early glow, that concupiscent, or what men had taken for concupiscent, sheen. She looked tired and dowdy, unhappy in cheap fashions of weeks rather than months, run up from thin fabric which came apart, like paper, at hems or seams, creased and tore, but could not, on her budget, be replaced as often as was required. No more than her hair could be trimmed and blown dry once a week. The sixties, like the eighties, were cruel in defining affordability, while Elisabet would smile wryly when reading, as she often did, in tabloids and women's magazines, that, actually chic could be cheap. This is a nonsense: what self-regarding woman *wants* her chic to be cheap?

Fortunately, fashion has this circular or spiral motion, so all was not lost. Not yet. Better times came with the lapse of the decade, the ageing of its progenitors, the threshold of recession, with hippiedom, flower power, the gentle, penniless, loving, dropped-out people. Now you could dress like Asians in thin, light material made from a bedspread, in see-through cottons and cheap Victoriana. The older and tattier the better. Elisabet purchased granny specs and an army greatcoat to wear over thin dresses. With her soft looks, soft flesh, long true-blonde hair and the abstraction in her pale-blue eyes, as skint as the poorest but living much better than she had for years in several organised squats, large scrubbed houses, ex-rectories, surgeries and so forth, waiting to be renovated by the council, Elisabet felt regenerated, yes, almost redeemed. She had begun to grasp that life, which must be plotted against the political and social climate, is, however quietly, always in transition between points. But she had not understood what a declining trend her own pattern followed; she knew only that something had just peaked, that for the moment her sense of the present fitted.

It was a peaceful, grass-smoking, largely macrobiotic period, in which her maternal curves were well set off by richly printed cottons tucked over mattresses in tidy, if gappy rooms, whose bells, wind chimes, silk scarves, posters, candle flames, and small appendages of Buddhist shrines always seemed to be in motion in the draughts through unstopped floors and ancient windows, and where she enjoyed, in a new way, the attentions of young men who liked having an older woman in bed. So young, some of them had barely left school. They wore pony tails, sprouted fuzz rather than beards, brewed constant pots of tea spiced with a herb that threw fine smoky veils over what could otherwise have been uncomfortableness.

The lovers came and went, but this happened to everyone. The nature of the period was to be transient, mercurial, so laid-back that anything other than 'unlaidbackness' passed. The homes were sometimes as short-term as her lovers, starting up or closing down in a matter of days, but this was fine, this was all in order; it was, as they said, *cool*. And it did not matter that her companions were as transient as they were rootless and generous, for, interestingly, in the peeling kitchens and naked hallways and ritualistic rooms, meeting and losing house-mates almost every day, but always with a spontaneous cuddle and kiss, she experienced her first real warm sense of family.

It did not even matter about her hobby. You told everyone everything in those days, so she made no secret of her arduous scribbling. It was in her third squat that Elisabet had made her second firm decision. She was now working at a novel which was supposed to capture, she could not quite explain how – genius cannot be described in one sentence – the spirit of the age. She had reached that stage when not only should existence be justified by goods or deeds, but an intelligence unsupported by power or university degrees must otherwise be proved. This was the reasoning behind her decision. She had, therefore, quickly to set about that proof.

It was hard work, writing, and financially draining (paper, typewriter, typewriter ribbons, so much paper!), and because of the learning factor, and what appeared to be the intractability of talent, disappointing at first. To support it, to justify money drawn out as dole, she still looked for work, typing, filing and so forth, work which was growing much scarcer, work for which the lean, aggressively suited girls in agencies indicated Elisabet was 'just not right'. They did not say so, of course, they merely looked at her soft face, her flowing hair, her fluid clothes, and clicked their sharp heels across the floor to apply the ridiculously difficult typing test.

The phone in the squats that had hardly ever rang in order to offer work. In the daylight the young men played guitar, or pursued second degrees, and Elisabet had quantities of spare time for revising, for fair-copying her manuscript – activities on which she grew to depend, for as she grew better at handling language, so she became personally more decisive, less amorphous. Only she could not make her novels (at first it was only one, then several, unpublished novels) any more like V. Woolf's than she could make them like Mailer's or Drabble's; her products, as she realised later, were too spiritual and fey, depending for their merits on high degrees of creativity, very elaborate images through whose richness could just be glimpsed, like a naked woman among gauzy layers, a minimal, in-determinate form. But the images were the thing. She had a very deep, unique supply – was astonished at how easily they came to hand, reams of them, fifteen, twenty pages a day, more if she smoked, twitching at the structure, or what passed for it, later. Why wasn't this facility, with descriptions, impressions, and so on – rather than boring old 'telling' – a mark of that genius which was, actually, so hard to discover it was often, especially by publishers, overlooked – missed?

Elisabet was so scornful of 'establishment' she almost did not send her manuscripts out. Only she did, because closet writers can expect neither remuneration or what they really covet – Elisabet did not think she was alone in this – fame.

In 1974 Father died cleanly from a heart attack as he was Turtle-waxing his elderly Austin, leaving, as he had threatened, and Elisabet had not believed, the whole of his estate to Eleanor.

Difficult times began. Eleanor's dutiful grief,

having a field day with an anxiously thin frame and unstretched constitution, produced, within a year, a mild stroke followed by the onset of Parkinson's, debility which Elisabet, affecting a blanket, some might say insensitive innocence, depending on her child-like clothes and vacant stare, could not finally ignore. She tried, but neighbours wrote. Eleanor's doctor wrote. The vicar phoned. Her brittle self-defence, her hopeful investment in transcendentalism, crumbled and discovered, underneath, that stratum of dutifulness which persists as stoutly as sedimentary rock, no matter what you do with the topsoil.

How costly caring is! But at least Mother paid for the train fares. There were many journeys over the years, each renewing an adolescent anguish as the train slowed for the Surrey station from which Elisabet had made many wistful shopping trips, London, Meccawards, and from which, at last, at 9.43 one Sunday morning she had effected her Great Escape. Not irrationally, she now associated the sense of being trapped, and other less specific miseries, with heavy rhododendrons, lissom ferns, half-strangled silver birches, and the gassy smell of sandy soil and rotting mast – the sort of vegetation flourishing round the station and enclosing the last miles of track. It was not just imagination – a writer now, she scrupulously checked impressions.

More smells, even less pleasant, inhabited the old home along with Eleanor, clung to her, followed her, but also, in a curious amoebic kind of division, lingered in the chair or sofa where she'd been sitting; lay in the hollow in her unmade bed; hung with her coat in the hall. Unwashed clothes, barely washed plates, smeared crockery littering the draining-board; the dull-blue satin quilt impregnated with sick; an almost unspeakable bathroom; staleness in the passages; and a funny damp coldness rising through the feverish heat of the front room where Eleanor sat in her outdoor coat all day, the gas fire on full – 'getting Mother sorted', as Elisabet put it, was an ugly period of imprecise edges and ends, in the middle of which, hideously linking the seventies with the eighties, sat, very much like a wizened, baleful toad, the only half-rational but in no way dying Eleanor.

Retrospection did not dull, time did not amend, the horrible aspects of that era. Finding a nursing home, persuading the etiolated Eleanor – whose personality had reduced, along with her body, like a sharp but cloudy sauce – to accept, to sign papers, more papers, eventually to move, exhausted and worried Elisabet. What was her young man with the pony tail and second degree doing while she was away? She might also have done other things than arrange for care, things concerning the sticks of furniture and other objects lying uselessly about. Might have, if they had not been charged with ugly histories, while her squat, in the throes of anti-possessiveness, carried on a brave, resourceful existence among scrounged sticks of furniture and queerly draped windows, their cooker and fridge rescued from dumps, while other items ... It seemed there was some confusion about the difference between *found* and *stolen* or the 'not wanted' of a derelict house and that which was, actually, being refurbished. But they needed nothing, so when the time came Elisabet let the whole lot go, barely noticing where it ended up, or if everything was paid for.

The point at which she stalled, and over which, having failed, wept so many tears, was that the house must be sold in order to pay for Mother's nursing, in the only home that would accept Eleanor's exacerbating personality and incontinence. This was the wrenching, expensive alternative to coping alone; the provision was clearly set out in Father's will. The money must be used for care until Eleanor died. So there, again, one paid for being an undutiful, unwatchful daughter. The house probably went for less than it was worth. Elisabet, defeated by law, just took the first offer. Other resources, unwisely reinvested (for no reason but that, at her

worst, Eleanor was meddlesome and erratic) –
the stocks and shares so carefully built up by
Father – had dwindled to small, scattered,
unprofitable holdings which had, occasionally
(nickel, a collapsed retail outfit), been lost. And
now this illness, this slow, increasingly debili-
tating and therefore increasingly expensive
illness which, at the same time as it worked at
her mother's body, continued the business of
evaporating, calcifying her character, to such an
extent that, after some years, there was nothing
in the shrivelled, demanding but almost inert
person in Eleanor's bed (it must be her mother –
they told her it was) to link into, to remind her of
a vanished relationship. There was only a
tossing, intense, unfocused mental activity
within a twitching but useless body – which, in a
way, was a metaphor for how Eleanor had lived:
personality as denied by suburban conventions as
the spark in her brain was by a failure of muscle
and nerve.

So why visit? There seemed so little point – they
did not even look at each other, or take hands –
that one dull, wet Sunday in the winter of 1985
Elisabet resolved never to visit again. She really
could not bear the pain or futility; and there was
more pain involved in counting how much this
care was costing, how much it had already cost,
how much, or little, would be left at the end *if* it

went on much longer. If. The logarithm again. Elisabet was to get the residue *if* Eleanor – harsh admission, but crimes are committed for less – *if Eleanor died in time.*

This is what it came down to, then. She did not know exactly how much remained in the bank, but even for a scrap, she deserved *something*, would have ended her mother's life then, on the cold, intensely depressing day of her last visit. It was only a question of finding the means to do so. She looked hurriedly round the room. The move must have been anticipated – perhaps she was not the first visitor to feel so desperate – for there was nothing at all like a makeshift weapon lying about, no string or flex, no scalpel or syringe, not even a sewing needle, only soft, friendly innocuous objects, and not many of those. She would have, then, to use the pillow from which Eleanor's hard eyes stared and on which her small head, with its cap of tight, dry pincurls, endlessly rotated.

And she would. She would do it. Here was something to confound that obdurate stare, that mouth which, through no fault of its own, had settled into a downturn of bitterness. Elisabet, flushed with decisiveness (there, that will surprise you, she thought), moved forward, raised her hands – but not enough to incriminate herself when, as if precisely cued, a nurse rattled the door handle and walked in with a quivering cup of tea. Surely Elisabet had only been there five minutes? Yet here, already, was her tea. And though, smiling warmly, she contrived to be left again, somehow the nurse insinuated herself, was in, out, propped the door open, called from the corridor where she had left a trolley inconveniently parked . . . Also, there was the indictment in Eleanor's eyes, which followed her cleverly around the room, which must have signalled, somehow, to the nurse. Eyes which looked game enough to survive – almost anything. Their look had changed, Elisabet had not imagined it; their look had changed when she lifted her hands and stepped forward . . .

After some minutes, having drunk her tea, Elisabet left, her only revenge being the absence of either goodbye or kiss, and the resolve never again to return. As she did not, though Eleanor, at the cost of some £10,000 a year, continued to live.

Heartless? No. An exigency to which Elisabet was reduced. It was not her fault. She did not know whose it was, but not hers. She was in straits again, returned, with the beginning of a new financial climate, to the state of mind experienced less sharply some twelve or fifteen years before: the nagging daily compare and contrast; horribly petty, demeaning budgeting; and the coping with pride which barely survives, so ugly is making do.

In nightmare fashion, time's moving pavement was conducting Elisabet to the weighty end of forty. It showed in her face and laxer figure, tragedy enough. But for the kind of work to which she was used, or had been used, before word-processors and electronic typewriters, her face, clothes, general dreamy manner and history of ignominious job-hunting no longer suited, except on the most menial levels where hardly anything mattered. Yet she had to work. Benefit payments go only a small way; they are calculated in the manner of Micawber's 20s 6d in the pound – necessary expenditure being almost always greater than the income they represent.

The novels, put aside during Mother's illness, had come to nothing. She did not pick them up, stopped mailing them for years, though they travelled alongside the rest of her belongings to increasingly meaner addresses, filling one large suitcase. Once, in a moment of inspiration, she abandoned the box containing the duplicates, copies much buffeted by travels to and returns from publishers, in a curtained-off recess in an attic in Clapham, feeling after as good as losing a stone in weight. She never thought of them again.

On another day, in more sober mood, she would do the same with the case of originals. Unless . . .? Hopes do not die if they are worth the name; they lie down and get ill, they go very quiet, but they rarely die. With nothing to do, and the light of that limpid summer evening gentling her view of the metropolis from a small second-floor room, she unsnapped the suitcase and, taking out a manuscript at random, began leafing through. Surprisingly, it wasn't bad. None of the novels, which she looked at casually, reading a paragraph here, a few sentences there, was awful. Elisabet, though difficult, stubborn, had never been stupid. But they weren't – there were five, she had written very fast, prodigal with that lush imaginative vein – as she saw more clearly now, good enough to be published by a firm that wants to make money. They had parts, many parts, but, as it were, there was not one good sum among them.

Still, with objective editing, some re-writing . . .?

Wisely or not – these are answers luck or determination supply, and Elisabet had abandoned both sources – she put the manuscripts back and closed the suitcase. It was not the right time. The summer sky had darkened, it looked like thunder, and the couple next door had begun making loud, percussive love: the shared plywood partition was shaken by their bed end, while their small compartment, the same size as Elisabet's (a Victorian guestroom chopped in half), echoed with other, more intimate noises. This, as it signalled an end to thinking, marked the problem which had contributed to the lapse in her writing. It was never easy to find quiet these days. Quiet, Elisabet inferred, is something the urban poor should not expect. They cannot afford it, cannot manage to live anywhere except cheek by jowl, and if they want peace, quietude, intellectual pleasure – well, there are sheltering parks, there are, as many oddballs know, the reading-rooms in public libraries.

So she did not knock on the vibrating wall, which would have been intrusive and censorious. She did not much like the couple next door, but pitied their lack of privacy for an occupation becoming almost memory to herself. They were of mixed origins. The boy, pasty-faced, Polish-surnamed, was really more gentle than he appeared – it was only his haircut which was intimidating – while she, slightly lighter than Asian, or an extraordinarily wheat-skinned Asian, was pretty, with a Birmingham accent so strong Elisabet thought that that must be the reason why she did not want to talk.

They, or rather the boy, had told her one morning of deploring the inadequate facilities, a pipe had burst in the single lavatory – that they were on the waiting-list for a flat, or little house. But so were several hundred other families in their district; they had been waiting for two years and there was no sign of a vacancy. Besides, the girl confessed, in a way they almost dreaded to be moved: the estates for which they were destined were run down, vandalised, and notorious for racial violence.

The small, quiet wife with her almondy, astigmatic eyes was terrified of being left alone. Even at night, she whispered, they would not be safe. There were petrol bombs, letter-box arsonists, people who heaved concrete through windows and smeared faeces on walls, were there not?

In a way, though cramped and longing to start a family, for which there was no space, they were better off here where, homeless (they did not call their cubicle home), no one thought they were stealing anything. An irony, for who really wanted the space they would eventually be given?

Elisabet listened with sympathy. She could bear to listen less, though she did, to some of the other blustering tenants. Without escape plans, or resources, or, indeed, anything to look forward to, she found her capacity for sympathy curiously expanded. It was as if she had to hurt herself, to feel how others hurt. In the days of being better off she had not cared. Now, without ability to help much, other than to listen, and being increasingly wounded, because she was down and without friends, she began to smart for others' pains.

This was how she met Napoleon, how she

allowed him to fall in with her, a strange, oldish-young man with, she thought, a touch of schizo-phrenia – a harmless eccentric whom once she would have passed on the other side of the street. She had come, some months before, to the small bedsit in Victoria. It was dingy and dirty when she arrived, but at least it had, through a large bay window, a north view of a depressed-looking park. Well, perhaps park was a euphem-ism – it was only a piece of open ground fronted by two barish flowerbeds and, further in, darkened by sycamore and planes. Nevertheless, the grass belonged to the darker scale of green tones, and in the spring and summer stunted flowers appeared in the sticky beds. There was also a railing bounding the park, and a gate which shut at night. These small observations, of nature answering to seasons and of temporal, hopefully behavioural, restrictions, offered some solace.

There was plenty of time to look for solace, for finally she had nothing to do. Occasional work was exactly that: waiting at tables, operating a till, packing shelves with iced buns, covering for sickness and holidays. The positions never lasted; they led nowhere. Used to re-ceiving her dole and to using her dwindling savings to eke it out, for a while she accepted what she ironically felt was her lot – less the lot she had chosen than the one which, through no fault of her own, had been handed out.

She did not notice exactly when it was that she began to lose hope – not hope for a glamorous future, that had long gone, but hope for an improvement in the situation. Nowadays so many people appeared to have so much! Young people too, even more than twenty years ago. Elisabet was staggered by the height of prices, the range of attainable goods, the number of large, very powerful cars whisking down London streets, creating large bow-waves of water or dust, while she herself seemed to have joined those rarely smiling people about whom every detail signifies not only that they have little or nothing (that nothing looking like a minus compared to abundance elsewhere) but that they have next to no prospects too.

Since between occasional official appointments ('Just checking your records' – insincere smile, or no smile, as if she were somehow culpable), between the odd day or two of work or attempts to get work (which, actually, after the expenses of travel, left her worse off, so she was less inclined to try for it – just as she was disinclined, it was too much trouble, to apply for travel subsidies) she had little to do, Elisabet read and thought a great deal about her problem. About *the* problem. She even read Marx, and one or two other theorists. Her conclusions left her even sadder. What she found only confirmed what she had more than suspected, had known without verbalising it: Elisabet, like Napeoloen, was not an individual casualty (not individual at all, except to herself) but just unlucky enough to become part of that residue which every era shrugs off. People may write books, conditions may improve (today's poor are not as poor as the poor used to be), but it is clear that certain, not luxuries, but requirements will remain beyond the reach of some; they must, unless they are supplied at less than profitable rates. Heating, for instance. It is almost impossible, if you are unemployed, to sit at home all day during the long cold season and keep both solvent and warm. Similarly, telephones are out, as are good leather, rubber-soled shoes. This list may go on: services and merchandise cost, while profit margins will never be large enough to allow of charitable dispensation (where would you start; how will 'these people' Micawber *et al*, ever learn if you do?) simply because profits, unlike loaves and fishes, are never large enough for all who want their cut.

The century was not enlightened after all, and Elisabet, who had omitted to heckle, thrust, bargain for herself, had joined that number who are always the ladder's essential bottom rung, the negative by which the lucrative position, the positive image, is proved: metaphorically, the mirror in which the rich man admires his gold watch, his immaculately crowned front teeth, his silk suit. Elisabet was not personal, for waste is not that, any more than constants, like light, water, food, and heat, are things that should be much considered. Not even a cork in an ocean, she was just one atom of a toxic sea which cannot be skirted or bridged, if you reach its shore; and which, if entered, is so much harder to leave. Such, Elisabet thought, *en masse* are the poor.

5

... and when at last I did see a turnkey (poor little fellow that I was!), and thought how, when Roderick Random was in a debtor's prison, there was a man there with nothing on him but an old rug, the turnkey swam before my dimmed eyes and my beating heart.

May 1989

Elisabet could therefore see how she had ended up with nothing. (She could see, that is, how she had been foolish not to invest, to save; to have relied on the vagaries of fortune for security; and to have not become effectively reconciled with her father, receiving, as reward, a portion of his estate.) She could not argue with the reasons. But it was less easy to accept (because ending up is so desperately final) with slightly over £50 to fall back on, in a bedsit from which, it seemed, there was no escape. In the spring she had tried not to whittle her savings below the £100 mark, but had quickly failed. Soon she would have gone right through the £50. What then?

Having felt so capable when trying to help Napoleon, she felt, conversely, incapable when she thought of her own dilemma, lying prone on her bed, memory valve opened to the warmth of summer, recollections flowing, her discomfort as bad as if they were nails on which she reclined. She felt in the same spot as someone with bad toothache: the pain made her probe. Perhaps she was looking for a secret spring, a hitherto concealed fact, the discovery of which, as the royal birthmark in a fairytale, would cause her life to change? A fantasy created as much by panic as by sheer apathy, because she was teetering on that edge down which Napoleon, so long ago now, had helplessly, inevitably slipped.

Indeed, he seemed to be disappearing from reach. For days on end she lost sight of him. He drifted along the river banks, that much she knew, sometimes further, into the city parks, east beyond St Paul's or north, around Russell Square, the areas where he slept often noisy, violent, making him afraid. Being disturbed disturbed Napoleon; he appeared to be even less sensible, blundering in a fogged mental landscape from which he would not egress to talk to Elisabet. She feared for him even as her worst fears began to come true. Shorn of vital bits and pieces, of the topography of personal habitation, he was, past floundering, beginning to drown. For there was nothing by which he could mark his place in the world. Everywhere, he complained to her, he tried to establish his bedding and occasional cardboard coffin, he had been usurped or blackmailed or robbed – yes, cheated of just a few shillings by someone tougher. He had been cleaned out countless times. Today he did not bother to own anything except the clothes in which he stood. Not even a blanket. It was also obvious that he did not, ever, wash.

With the last flush of blossom gone, and a fine green wash spreading over the park trees, a wash which almost overnight took on substance and a third, deeper dimension, as if someone, painting furiously, had started with outline, suggestion, but was moving on to depth, Elisabet realised she had not seen Napoleon for more than three weeks. His last appearance, after several days spent sleeping, for reasons she could not understand, among alcoholics in a bandstand in Bloomsbury, had shocked her. Gaunt, offensively smelly, his eyes apparently unfocusing as they slid in her direction, he had barely remembered who his friend was. His breath was loaded with spirits; it brought his words to her in a repellent fug from which she turned instinctively as he swayed in slow, even rhythm from side to side for the short time she had him upright. On the bench where she eventually seated him it was hardly better; he wanted only to sleep. No money, of course: she confirmed this by looking in his pockets, a disgusting act but necessary. Whether he had claimed his last benefit and drunk it, or not claimed it at all, or only been robbed again, Elisabet was unable to discover.

Yet even in this horrible state, one which seemed less like Napoleon than a badly acted version of him, a part of his unforgetting self materialised at the back of his eyes; spoke to her, beckoned from a long way off. Poor Napoleon. The drink did not, would not ever suit him – obviously he had been intimidated into it. He was neither merry nor raucous, but numb, and that, she supposed, was why, once drunk, he drank again. Amnesia, in that sense, was kind.

Finally, as she was leaving, he was extravagantly sick. Elisabet heard the first stages as she was some fifty yards away, and turned. Napoleon, supporting himself on a railing, retched and spat, stooping so that the reticulations of his thin spine, and the wave-like stresses of each spasm, were clearly visible. But, outside the park already, she did not start back. What, she asked herself, very reasonably, could she do?

Her friend had reached a state which was beyond aid, because he was no longer interested in aid. Help meant change, and that was now more uncomfortable than the status quo. As long as he drank and sometimes ate something, for which there was usually some sort of charitable provision, what else could anyone do? (Elisabet, not wishing to ape the arguments of politicians, found herself doing just that.) What Napoleon needed was not just the sustenance of soup and sandwich runs. He needed drying out, cleaning up, reordering, housing – and? She found herself outlining a very daunting programme, one which ought, really, to reach for the soul, and whose success, therefore, was not certain. She could see how 'they' saw it. Napoleon, in a kind of Mephistophelean bargain, had wilfully blinded himself to good judgment, self-help, assertion, all these modern, thrusting, energetic techniques, in order to reach a position which was the complete opposite to that being politically intended.

Of his own free will, as they put it?

Does anyone really will to be as an orphan, looking through windows at the plenitude of the party from which he or she is excluded?

Elisabet, back home, studied the dismal figures in her building society book and did not think so. She thought that all that might be freely willed is a swift or boozy end to a painful situation which, in Napoleon's case, looked like a cul-de-sac from which he had neither energy nor enough understanding to reverse.

While she was still trying to hold on to her friend, trying to trace him among tourists and lunchers who suddenly filled the parks and from whose affluence she believed he fled, more problems cropped up. Her electricity bill came, and somehow it was Napoleon's fault that she had forgotten to put money aside since the last quarter. And not only that. She had actually spent money on his behalf every week since he had become homeless, in addition to buying small comforting luxuries for herself, drawing heavily on her savings. Now they wanted from her the sum of £89.23, while she had just £51.91 left. And how, she asked bitterly, could she spend that on heat she had already consumed? Savings are for that which is not entirely necessary, for treats, luxuries, etc. But for heat? For cooking, water, light. *Savings*?

As anyone would, Elisabet ignored the bill until the red warning arrived. A small, punishingly bright piece of paper, it made the obvious threats. She must take steps and quickly. It was as if the red print had some quality, invisible before, enabling her to see her kettle dead, her light bulb out; hardly had she ripped it from the envelope than she began to sweat. With some fortitude, she thought, action was taken: phone calls, visits made in person. The unmatronly, drably clothed woman behind the desk was patient but firm. She still used, expected to use electricity, didn't she? Then she must pay for what she had already consumed, or they would stop her consuming what she had not paid for: therms not included in that bill which were even now adding to her debt.

'But it's money management,' the young,

smart counsellor, to whom Elisabet had been referred by the benefit office, said. Together they went through her budget, a beautiful piece of deceit which made unfair assumptions about the prices of things, taking for granted that Elisabet needed neither travel, entertainment nor even money to buy newspapers. It pretended, in fact, that it could nourish, heat and cook on a little over £30 a week. In London! Obviously, the food must be of the barest, the cooking of the scantiest (no ovens) and – luckily it was warm – bar fires were not to be thought of. It went without saying that Elisabet did not have, had lately never had, the right to buy stockings, or paper on which to scribble things, or postage stamps, or replacement underwear, or lipstick, or hairgrips, or (as often) settle crippling library overdues.

'Try the WVS,' the counsellor, who had a very new, long full perm (£50 worth?), said evenly as her pencil moved down the list.

'Try walking.'

'Try not respiring?' Elisabet asked tartly.

'What?'

'Trite, but true. Not even breathing's free,' Elisabet murmured (the counsellor was writing and gave no sign that she had heard). It requires energy – she continued the thought in her head – for lungs and heart, and muscles need energy to work, and where does that energy come from? From food.

'You really should try and find some work,' the counsellor said at the end of the interview, having tucked the shortfall on Elisabet's budget sheet away in a cardboard file. Her pencil had hovered over the red, undisciplinable amount for a moment. Clearly she would have liked to strike it out, for only Elisabet's incomings were government concern; how they matched with her outgoings, except according to mean, rapidly outdated tables, was not.

'Inflation,' Elisabet said, 'is around 8 per cent.'

The counsellor sighed. It was 5.43 and she would be going somewhere tonight.

'Well,' she said briskly, 'we are all in the same boat. We'll just have to tighten our belts a little more. At a pinch there are . . .' Elisabet thought she was about to say money-lenders. Her mouth contracted, as for an 'm', when it was checked and turned into what Elisabet thought was called a *moue*. 'And there are various other one-off benefits.' She passed across a leaflet, the classic put-down. 'Look through these to see if any apply. And come back and see me . . .' – her hands flipped through a wad of spacious diary pages – 'next month. Here, I'll write it down for you.'

Elisabet was too nicely behaved to leave the leaflets on the desk. Instead she dropped them in a bin on the way out. She had read them all before; they were full of platitudes, cosmetic dogma, underlining what she already knew – that there were actually far more tricky rules to negate the supposed benefits on offer than there were rules to make them apply. This snakes and ladders system, rich in penalties and thin on rewards, would be funny were it not both so damaging to people's hopes and so scandalously pious on its own behalf.

'So that's it.'

On the steps of the government building Elisabet paused to draw a shallow, not highly oxygenated breath.

Well, she had £51.91 anyway. But much more than that amount was now demanded by an electricity bill she therefore could not pay, and had no intention of trying to pay.

In the summer it is not too bad to be without light and heat. Elisabet, her supply disconnected, could make pretty if expensive salads. She enjoyed arranging the greens, reds and purples of lettuce, cucumber, tomatoes, beetroot in a blue or yellow dish, the whole garnished with studs of halved, boiled eggs, which made her think of ox-eye daisies and buttercup fields (did she dare buy a train ride to the country? No, theft apart, that meant more inroads, treats while there; she saw the £51.91 wobble, shrink . . .) or the waxy nasturtium-coloured shreds of grated cheese, not too much, because it was costly. On a rainy day she would add brilliant grated carrot, shreds of bitter, bright marigold snipped from the pot on her sill, Provençal olives. These meals further impoverished her. To eat properly, which is what the Department of Health, if not her own doctor, who did not care, would have her do, having lately spent money telling her to do this, was not cheap, especially as she could no longer cook and run up tasty little numbers from lentils and spuds. (Did dieticians ever work out how much cooking costs? Did they even think about it?) The bleak alternative to salads was to live on sandwiches and unheated, cheap unnutritious gristle pies

Sometimes she ate dismally, worse than pies, melanges of horrible leftovers at the table for one, looking on to a quadrilateral section of park, entertaining sad comparative memories of abundant lunches at her parents' table, that period in the fifties when she had never counted the cost of provisions which always included plenty of meat, fish and fruit, which had been very kind to the palate if looking rather dull. The vision, it seems, needs much more of a treat when you're down.

At least it was hardly ever cold. When it was she wrapped herself in the old pink quilt and tried to read. What she missed most was a hot drink – obviously, no power means no kettles, and although she tried befriending a neighbour or two, in the hopes that they would heat some water, these efforts came to nothing. The neighbours were either as odd and suspicious as Napoleon had become, or frankly uninterested, or always out.

Occasionally, when desperate (hot tea was by far the cheapest way of lifting spirits – her counsellor would approve), an ancient woman who lived in the basement in a room piled with old newspapers obliged, though Elisabet was afraid of her dirty hands and the contents of a smeared kettle. Once a sharp young girl whom she guessed worked as a prostitute supplied a jugful. There were no local friends. What acquaintances she thought she still had were scattered over different districts to which she could hardly afford the fare. If she had visited, they might have filled a thermos flask for her return. A ridiculous expense. Also, she had, as proportion and a sense of economics began to fail, no flask.

It was hard not to cry when she saw herself managing like this, eventually treasuring a stopperless vacuum jar found in a skip. (For no, she would not dip into the £51.91 for a flask, for anything yet; there was a sort of superstition attached to the roundish, intact sum.) Religiously cleaning the jug at home, she improvised a stopper from foil and felt absurdly pleased.

There – that had cost nothing at all! Now she could make the process of scrounging water a daily one, exultant whenever she found a new outlet – a sympathetic café, an immaculate housewife on whose door she boldly knocked. On these journeys, she sometimes picked up other items – a newspaper from a bin, a comb dropped on the station steps, a coin, odd gloves poised on railings like severed heads. It was a natural development, and though sometimes she recoiled in horror – was this really Elisabet, Elisabet Stern? – she did not drop the habit. Everything found, not bought, became, need notwithstanding, a treasure with which she scurried home, experiencing inklings that she was already entering Napoleon's 'state of un-ordinariness', the tip-tilted idea that she, as observer, had witnessed, long before he spoke of it, in his uncanny, loving relationship with the odd, borrowed, scrounged, stolen items of his squat.

She had thought then that what he had spoken of, in the café by the river, described home-lessness only. Now she saw (quickly – she did not look hard, was anxious to deny an idea that returned, returned) that it belonged to that precariousness when home, while existing, is not what the common idea holds it to be; and when homelessness, though not actual, not yet, is so close it leans on every thought, seems to prowl like some ominous hybrid, a childish nightmare, in the street, has as much disturbing force, presence, physicalness as the bailiff, with whom, perhaps, it will, as it threatens to so frequently, come.

Yet even when she came down to the point when she wanted, was entitled, to cry, was prepared to open the valve, she found only a parched dryness, a few flakes of rust, perhaps, a sense of plumbing being stretched but nothing further emerging from that tap whose failure – she thought it might be a little like problems with urination – only added to the overall discomfort.

Nights were the hardest – lightless times when she tried to sleep and could not, for a young ex-dosser with a grim face and six rings in one ear, moving into the bedsit next to hers, had brought a powerful cassette-radio combine. The noise, worst at night but also infrequently during the day, added to her pain. She felt her sanity slipping with the mindless bass frequencies which reached her, relentlessly, whatever the volume of the treble's apparently senseless language.

About all of which the ex-dosser would not be approached. To try was to be deluged with abuse, thrown at her like cold water over a troublesome cat, or even (because he gave rise to this line of thinking) hot over a troublesome baby. The young man was the child-basher kind, that was sure.

Shivering under her quilt, more from fear than from cold, in the light of the two candles by which she could just make out a portion of her page, and with cotton wool in her ears, she regretted that she could no longer cry. Weeks passed. Still she was unable. Her body must have guessed weeping would be no help; instead it tortured her with images, baked, cracked, fluidless images, visions of an inner wasteland which, she dimly remembered, had some echoes in something she had once read. Wasteland. Didn't that mean a singular patch of no-place, contingent on other bright areas which served to show it in relief? A no-hope area whose *real* hopelessness lay in its inability to furnish redemption, hope, escape?

What hope – she did not ask for redemption, just some help – what hope was left for Elisabet?

If only she *could* hope.

If only there was an attainable point to hope for.

And yet she felt, or had felt, so young!

Until she touched her face again, and found it not so young.

She looked awful these days. The efforts to get jobs were useless. She did not bother to mend her clothes. Had only cold water in which to wash her hair – so mostly did not bother. Her lipstick was finished. She did not replace it. Her nails grew, and broke, and were forgotten. She did not clean them. Her last pair of stockings had long ago laddered. She went about with pale bare legs, unshaved. Why remove the black hairs? Who would look?

When had a man last looked at Elisabet?

One, then two of her teeth began to hurt, but she did not go to the dentist. There just seemed no point.

As there was no point, also, in thinking about what to wear. She put on anything, the nearest things to hand; never mind the colours, or whether her clothes were dirty or creased. The washeteria was another expense she tried, as aften as possible, to avoid. Underwear could be washed in cold water and dried in her room, but dresses soaked the carpet as they dripped and cut out the light. Besides – again – who cared?

She clung on to the £51.91. It was her straw, her depression's raft, and as long as she kept it intact she felt that the evils which had swallowed Napoleon could not seize her. She had enough money to buy herself out of the next problem, whatever that might be (it was asking too much to enquire what lay *beyond* that next problem). She had, she repeated, enough money, enough money, in a rhythm to counterpoint the rhythm of the ex-dosser's, or brickie's (so someone had called him), radio next door. Privately, Elisabet thought he had less to do with bricks than with being stoned by a different material.

When his music drove her too mad she walked, whatever the hour, not caring what happened, thinking, anyway, that she seemed an unlikely proposition for a mugger. She was right. No one approached, though men seated with bottles on benches and walls made propositions she did not reply to. But the drunks did not alarm; they were incapable of much. They did not stop her walking until 3 or 4 a.m., seeing in the warm midsummer dawn on the way. The brickie might turn his music off then. Sometimes the silence went on into the first stirrings of street life, about 5 a.m., allowing her some fitful sleep through the first light hours or, if she was lucky, until as late as the afternoon.

Soon this prolonged dozing, it was never a good sleep, became a habit, and the days grew as muddled as her sense of time. She forgot, more than once, to sign on for her benefit and, through inertia, then left it so late to visit the office that she had to start it up all over again, with consequent, grave losses of money. Each time the rent, which was paid directly, was stopped.

Troubles, along with her arrears, mounted. Soon Elisabet, in increasingly rare periods of rationality, saw that she was losing her grip on those private and public rituals by which sanity and normality are determined.

What is the day today, Elisabet?

She did not always know.

What month is it?

She began to forget.

Have you claimed your benefit this week? *Is* it this week you claim your benefit?

She was not sure.

When do you claim again?

She claimed every Thursday fortnight. The weeks and part-weeks were increasingly difficult to calculate.

Lying on her bed, she would go cold with sweat when she realised how much her metaphorical fingers had loosened on the quotidian strand: dates, hours, meals, regularity, regularity. How long before, in the gradual disintegration which may become a slide, which may become an avalanche – unless it was like a large rubber, moving repeatedly but increasingly effectively over her brain's data – how long before even her own surname became detached?

How long before, to some group of drunks as much as to herself, she was only a hole for pouring booze in, and a body for having a go at? Shapless, dirty Beth, Bet, Lizzie, Liz.

Or plainer cunt, tart, crumpet, pussy. Bitch.

More plain, you. Her.

And at the end, *it, that.*

Body: name, provenance unknown.

No one could tell her exactly when Napoleon died, except the authorities to whom she did not go. Few remembered him anyway. Mike had disappeared, some said he had gone back home, and Darien was in jail for a string of offences which escalated – perhaps because he was already conveniently booked; though perhaps not – to a charge of rape. Nor could anyone say of what he had died, though Elisabet guessed it was a combination of alcohol, malnutrition and exposure. He had lasted such a short time, hardly five months, and it wasn't even cold! For his sake a few tears came, on a very bright September day as she drifted along the Embankment, looking at crowds of tourists. She supposed that these people represented current normality. To be normal was to be so spirited as to seem carefree; perhaps dressed in linen or cotton cut briefly at arms, hips, necks, in order to display and flatter bronzed skin. To be normal was to be with other people like yourself, busy prospering, getting on with, like ant or bee colonies, a fine corporate ignorance of other non-contiguous affairs.

Looking down into the oily river, she tried to picture her friend's long, thin face with its light shawl of hair; tried to remember it as it had appeared in the last mean place, the squat of which he had been so inordinately proud.

'From he that has not,' Elisabet whispered bitterly.

She wondered if he had been afraid at the end – if he had known it was the end – or only glad? Probably he had died in a stupor. It was possible that no one had known who he was, known no more, anyway, than the little his dossing-mates had been able to supply; than his benefit card, if extant, had furnished leads to. Elisabet knew nothing of his family – supposing there were members still living. She was most likely the only one able to bear witness to the fact that he had lived – lived in the fullest sense that he was able, rather than, as latterly, drifting, purblind, in a limbo. But at least that state had one value: it had both blurred, and prepared him for, what he must have guessed was going to come.

Could things really have been better? For him? For herself?

Stumbling along beside the river as she mourned her friend, she passed three groups of young beggars – a single and two pairs. One young man in a torn, filthy sweatshirt called after her, rudely threatening as she avoided walking close. She had already divided her widow's mite with Napoleon at a time – not so long ago, it was early spring – when he had been solid, had embodied a problem she had thought she could help. She had been wrong. So today, as if in spite, she did not spare even 5p. What good would that do anyway? The supplicants were young, tough. Charity, she had grown to understand, was so little obligatory as to be a matter of very selective choice. To be a matter of yes or no.

Today she felt a little more like the luckier ones who do the bulk of the choosing as she too decided *no*.

As if the electricity cut-off and Napoleon's disappearance were not enough, a crisis occurred with her tenancy. She had always thought that the property was owned by a charitable body; the rent was reasonable. But suddenly a new owner, a man with a multisyllabic name rich in vowels, appeared, announcing, in a densely printed letter, of which, she innocently assumed, everyone received a copy, that it was his intention to renovate all the bedsits and flats in the building, thereafter levying an 'adjusted' rent in order to reflect the cost of improvement. Also, it ran on – there were almost two pages of it, the print much smaller than usual – a service charge would be introduced, to accommodate a cleaning of hallways and landings (this must mean the end of the sluggish woman with the broom), attention to paintwork, central plumbing, and extensive repairs to the roof.

Another long paragraph tried to bluff with mention of sinking funds, additional liabilities, investments, built-in increments, ranges of percentages, but Elisabet, on her third, frightened read, was able to make out what, initially, seemed to have been overlooked. During improvements – the commencing date of which was found to be so horribly close it was only five weeks away, by which time all properties must be vacated, keys handed over – the tenants would of course, if they chose, be rehoused. The letter mentioned an address just off Commercial Road. No repossession, though, without two months of the new rent in advance.

Having spent an hour trying to calm herself, succeeding a little with her heart rate, Elisabet made one phone call to his office. A woman with a blurred accent, as mealy as couscous, whom Elisabet suspected of being the new owner's wife, answered. Oh yes, she said, smoothly, they hadn't the *exact* figures yet, but it appeared that the new rents would be somewhere between 'double and treble'. And no, she continued, just as if she had anticipated this question and done her research, Elisabet was not registered as a 'fair rent', was she? And neither would she be able to do this now, these practices being in the past. Had Elisabet not heard of the new Housing Act? The freeholder, she patiently explained, was entitled to request a market rent for his property. How do you think, she asked, her voice sharpening perceptibly, he can maintain it, a large, elderly building like that, while paying rates, etc., to make no mention of the *enormous* cost of improvements, as it stands? Had Elisabet any idea how much building work cost? With VAT added? What the running expenses were?

A pause, just long enough to register that, of course, Elisabet had no idea.

Oh, you can depend on it, the woman said, it was all within the law. Well within, actually. Improvements were always welcomed. But Elisabet was free to make enquiries. Quite free. Try your solicitor, the woman said. Or, she laughed, the DSS. Oh, and by the way – thus delivering the unexpected *coup de grâce* – they would be writing to her about the arrears.

Her hand still on the phone, though the woman had rung off, Elisabet was at first too stunned to move. She crunched the letter in her hand and leant her forehead on the phone booth's dirty glass. She did not understand it. She understood exactly what had been said, but these things could not happen. Surely not. Nowadays. And when, at last, on her blind walk, heading instinctively for the river – she certainly did not want to go home – some meaning emerged, she saw only that they wished to fool her, pretending that she did not know of the intricate structure of rights that protected her and her goods. They were trying to frighten, that was all; they were ignorant of her knowledge (Elisabet was careful not to be precise about this knowledge). It was easy, really. She did not need to be afraid. She would just . . .

But she had no time to be clear about what she would do – supposing she were able to be clear; she was already so muddled about so much – because, responding to the subtle menace of the letter, the crude impartiality of figures and dates, the ripple of muscle evident, despite the clever wordiness, in two stiff pages of pretty small print; responding also to the formless fear that she *might* be wrong, that in fact, nobody, the law least of all, could help, she at last, for the first time in weeks, began to cry.

'Dammit,' she stuttered, weaving inebriatedly in her path as the first tears came; she did not want her bedsit changed. (She stopped briefly at a litter bin, for there was a slipper sticking out, which she took.) Her way of life was awful, it was cheerless and lonely, and she recognised, through her fog, saw very sharply, in today's frightened clarity, that she was disorientated, that everything was getting worse. But she had a place. It was hers, she said, repeating Napoleon's last arguments; perhaps that's why they sounded both so pathetic and so heart-rending. Yet there was justice here. She had a right to that last little bit of history and security, an address called home; a right to preserve it too, as she liked and could afford. Home, just as it was.

Now that Elisabet had started to cry, she

could hardly stop. She spent days continuously weeping, while fear, held at bay even when reduced to candle, cold food, and daily, almost obsessive, scrounging, the fear first apparent when Napoleon lost his home, a fear then perceived as a stagnant, not too dangerous pool, glinted, rustled, drove a rush of concentric ripples against what she had always felt were good defences. It was as if someone had thrown a missile in, and continued throwing. The ripples came, abated, and came again, with promises of further disturbance. She heard their murmur in the nights as well as the days. In lulls she remained aware of imminent activity; fear, like allergy, needs only the first foothold to assure itself of continued accommodation, for sensitivity, that is its nature, nourishes to the extent of fabricating that which it most dreads.

At night, slapping outside Elisabet's nugget of candles, at the extremities of her cold limbs, the pond also had smell. It smelt so badly that she gagged, her mouth open, nostrils repudiatingly flaring and closing. When the brickie activated his music, its surface became hideously busy and sonorous.

She seemed always to hear jeers now. They came from the brickie's friends, who, when drinking, made feral noises, in which she detected not only bestiality but a more general unfeelingness. She thought frequently of gallows, guillotines, stocks; and censure by job, wallet, duped dense crowd mentality, a force vividly conjured for her by every indifferent, repulsed or just inquisitive glance that came her way; or the swell of acoustic nightmare, issuing, with a froth of oaths, from her neighbour's room. Neither would she believe that she was hallucinating: it seemed only that the last garments were dropping from a society in which she had foolishly put her trust; that shortly it would stand before her in its awful nakedness, proving that everything she had previously believed, everything interpreted from outward show, had been wrong. Just that. Wrong.

She had always thought, for instance, in the part of herself which denied an innate terror and prescience, that the soft area of amorphousness which absorbs nobodies – persons with less than no status, without homes or, apart from for official purposes, much of a name – that that swamp (there, – the term) would never really claim her. Something would intervene. Her mother still lived. Here was tie, identity, even though Eleanor, as they had informed her last year, being blind as well as deaf, was confined to a long night, edging towards death. Elisabet thought of her now as a bag of bones strung about with skin and a little flesh, an unsturdy coracle, drawn by the ebb. An assetless coracle too. The money had recently been exhausted, although, due to approaching demise, for which she would be hospitalised, Eleanor would not yet be moved.

For her, then – but what kind of bond or guarantee was this? – the slow tide waned towards its sunless horizon. Elisabet could not even grieve properly for Eleanor, or Napoleon – the music of her sleepless neighbour throbbed on, compounding her confusion, while in the street below her room, the dipsomaniac who had made his home in the little park howled. Perhaps he was singing at the moon, though Elisabet was reminded of something less light and more cheerless.

Neither could she put on the kettle to make tea, as the truth glared out horribly from patches when her fog lifted, nor read a book quietly, nor turn on the light. Not walking, barely moving, she lay on her divan's sour-smelling cover, ears attending to something they picked up beyond her neighbour's music: a low, creeping, nearing sort of sound, a kind of oncoming thunder, a sound which gradually filled, embattled, and still increased. It was, she thought once, how the oncoming tide must sound to the temporarily stranded shell; it was, she supposed, the fulfilment of what she had heard presaged by imaginary reeds and to which, on closer examination, her dying mother seemed to be drawing

her also . So this was it, this approaching powerful, inevitable . . . what? Has anyone found its
correct name? Come back, like Lazarus, armed
with glossaries, terms? A credible expansion?

As if required to submit, her mind, whatever
her efforts, refused sleep just as it stalled at
confrontation. Not even at dawn these days
could she doze. All daylight therefore became
super-bright, hallucinogenic, a kaleidoscopic
jungle of sound and form which she could not
manage to sort out. It was as if a cubist hand had
rearranged meaning, as Napoleon had compul-
sively rearranged the last meal she had bought
him, while Elisabet, even in her brightest moments, could not, did not want to, remember
enough to reassemble the pieces correctly. She
believed she had forgotten both what order
signifies and what disorder entails. But it did not
matter. In fact, at the moment, this seemed best.

6

'It is merely crossing,' said Mr Micawber, trifling with his eye-glass, 'merely crossing. The distance is quite imaginary.'

October 1989

Stepping out under the opaque vaults of the Gare du Nord, through which something less than daylight struggled, Elisabet recoiled from the heat. It must be overpowering in August. It was now October, and she felt she must have arrived in Africa, because of the stuffiness, the prevalence of sweat and other body odours. On the train which met the night boat, and which would have arrived hours ago had it not been for the inevitable difficulty – a go-slow at the docks – she had shared a carriage with drunks, students and two overtired families, whose children noisily complained, or just wailed, in a pitch very finely calculated by nature (calculated, that is, for greatest annoyance) when they did not sleep. It was the cheapest way to travel – what could you expect? The families and students ate continuously. Elisabet was amazed at the stores of damp-looking food regularly retrieved from carrier bags, rucksacks, collapsible hold-alls, even, on one occasion, a slim snap-shut handbag. Pretending offence, but really smothering her own hunger, she turned to watch the French night repeating itself in the train windows (the night seeming to hurtle like a strip of un-developed negatives through glass which apparently held itself still – how we minimise, she thought, the disturbance of travel) and wondered how often, in the future which in-cluded tomorrow, she would be able to afford to eat.

They had said that food was expensive here. Not as much as she had feared, but then, she had only settled on the station brasserie, that rather than a stand-up snack at the kiosk next door. Just one treat. It was past 8 a.m. and she had to have coffee. Two cups, and a baguette, with some runny *confiture* tasting only of sugar and colour, yes, she really did think it tasted bright orange. All this came to somewhat over 30 francs; she had been told she could get a room for only five times that amount – five times two small cups of not very hot coffee and a baguette which crumbled away to white powder when she bit or otherwise broke its hard crust. The comparison between costs of food and shelter here, in contrast with like comparisons in London, un-nerved her. She realised that, unlike Napoleon, with rent money set aside, she was more in danger of starving than sleeping out, a differential that would have pleased her late friend.

But why here? Why so exotically and, as some would have said, unrealistically, cross the Channel?

Before leaving, in the week before she was to vacate her flat (her recovery to some sort of sanity, a little peak on her declining graph, had come too late for anything but rough planning; or was it – for she still did not investigate possibilities of reversal – that the price of that sanity was to let the eviction process slide?). Elisabet had visited the last remaining friend from whom she did not feel entirely estranged – assumption based on the regularity of Christmas cards, and an occasional brilliant seaside view, with no less cryptic a message. How vestigial, how very much based on assumption, Elisabet was soon to think, friendships are!

Denise too had changed, had been cauterised, rather than tempered, by age. She looked scrawnier, hollower, harder, and was herself on the verge of a move. She was the only one left on an open landing where all the other flats had been emptied and boarded up. At the end of the day, she said – and this said a great deal, said it all – she would prefer it at Mum's.

Packing cases and cardboard boxes stood opened and partly filled in all her rooms. The curtains were already down. Nevertheless, there was a cup of tea, and that kind of interested (relieved?) sympathy accorded more willingly to those about to move their troubles out of reach. No sympathy so ready as that despatched with travellers.

Elisabet, explaining her plans to Denise, would have liked to endorse them with something clever, epigrammatic; would have liked to seem worldly, decisive; someone who had taken, as it first appeared, fate into her own hands. But it was hard to sound enthusiastic. Again, she was only playing victim, following the course bad management had opened. Eviction, which was what the landlord's manoeuvres amounted to, had not been her choice; neither, honestly, was escape abroad – *that* was simply a lesser evil.

The only effort made – she did not count the tremendous one of pulling herself out of the trough, just because she did not feel out of it for long – was in securing travel as an option, an optional luxury, one might say. To afford it, she had had to sell, in a long crawl round junk and antique dealers, almost everything she possessed.

'If I don't go now, I won't ever,' was how she put it. This sounded very lame and she cradled her cup so as not to see how Denise was trying, kindly, to look. Admiring? Concerned?

'But, Elisabet, as a foreigner, it will be much harder to get unemployment benefit.'

'And look, Elisabet, if you've spent absolutely everything . . .'

'Honestly, Elisabet, what are you going to *do*, once you're there?'

Although she thought that she was well rehearsed, she realised, when Denise put these questions, that she was as vague about facts as she had always been. She therefore shielded herself with generalities, referring, for instance, to the weather (it had been an unusually warm autumn so far) and the cheapness of accommodation. Remarkably, she could afford to stay in a modest hotel for about a week after she had paid her fare. She would live, she asserted, more confidently, on bread and apples, with a little cheese. She could live like that, happily, for a week, free as a bird. Here, she brightened. There was always a sense, in London, that the benefit people – to whom she reported every fortnight, who kept tabs, made notes – were monitoring every, albeit innocent, move.

She intended, she said, smiling, to enjoy the last of the sun, see some sights. Why, she had only ever been once, a long time ago, in the early sixties, to Paris. Only once!

What she did not add was that a young man with tinted granny specs who had struck up a conversation with her in the Embankment Gardens – they were both reading Russians, that was the link, his shiny and new, hers a backless semi-pulp found on the stairs – had said that begging in Paris was good, better than in London. She did not actually challenge this statement, because it was the kind of thing she wanted to hear, while imagination immediately dressed it up with implications about the sun's chemistry, generosity's vague relationship to open-air cafés, and an outdoor life which had made it easy to live all summer on almost nothing. Or so the young man said.

Elisabet, impressed by his browned appearance and confidence, felt proportion returning. So there *were* options? Not only that but, suddenly, miraculously, a plan. But she did not explain about the finer side, the begging, etc. to Denise; did not say that this was something she could face better in a strange country, where, stationed beyond the thoroughfares of old friends and acquaintances, anonymity was guaranteed. She could not bear to be found begging by a friend! Besides, she preferred to put herself at the mercy of Catholics, however lapsed. Making saints from martyrs, they surely understood the pain of abasement. They were also wiser about the needs of travellers: it was the young man who told her that hotels, even in the capital, were cheap.

So – this much she did tell her friend – since fate had made it so uncomfortable to stay here, she would see what it had arranged overseas.

The relief was apparent in Denise's face. At least, then, she had not come to impose herself, to initiate an unwelcome responsibility, to lean – perish the thought – on unhappy Denise, who was about to be forced out of her own place, such as it was. She glanced quickly at the stripped rooms, opening through opened doors from the kitchen in which they sat, as if to confirm she had lost almost as much as Elisabet. There were no curtains, hardly a stick of furniture remained. Had the bailiffs been? Though Denise's face was expressive of malcontent, she was vague about the circumstances. Funny, really, that Elisabet should choose to come, to say goodbye (Denise emphasised the goodbye), at this particular point. Why, if she'd chosen, say, next week, there'd be nothing but boards, and no one to direct her on.

The snag was, it was obvious really, that Denise could not possibly store the few things Elisabet had saved and would like to leave, pathetic relics which, she thought, hoped, did distinguish herself in quality, if not in plight, from Napoleon: the mother-of-pearl-backed hairbrush, the cushion made from a shabby kelim, the set of Dickens, two pairs of not irreparable shoes . . . navigational items which barely filled two boxes. There would be, Denise explained, what with all her own things, absolutely no extra room at Mum's. Sorry and all that, but . . .

125

Elisabet smiled weakly. She had not really expected anything. Yet it was not all sad. Denise's blanking off of the face on parting suggested a finality that was now welcome. She did not ask Elisabet to send cards, let her know how she was getting on. They would no more communicate than think of each other again. Elisabet, oddly, felt elation rising as she kissed the caked cheek and set off down the walkway, hearing the door close immediately in her wake, its slam another factor in her catalogue of freedom. Freedom from ties, interest, obligation, concern. An emotional bankrupt – you could not count Mother – she was glad she was liberated of the heart's, and of duty's, affairs, that she was finished, *outré*, connected with no one.

Or almost. After the last post had flopped through the door. After she had returned her key. Certainly, after the ferry had slipped from the dock. And look at all the paperwork, the cross-referencing, the persistent enquiries from which she was also about to be saved, Elisabet said, turning from the walkway into the first flight of dark stairs: the grid of forms and files (concerning tax, national insurance, unemployment benefit, social services, social security, health, rent, electoral role, etc.) which showed her name slotted in here, there (she imagined herself as some species of dull butterfly, pinned over and over, in drawers, files, card indexes, registers, computer systems, list after list), which, in their self-propagating, beadling manner, must periodically assure themselves of her existence, address, age, occupation and so on by sending out more forms which seemed both to generate and to cancel out themselves, enquiring and re-enquiring as to what she was doing, with whom, and where, if not there, then where, and when had she moved? – sometimes going so far as to summon her to interview, on a stamped, blurred date, with anonymous personnel; or requesting the reiteration of known details; or stating bluntly, as was more frequently the case, that, because of new regularly revised rules she would be receiving less of this, less of that, and must, to compensate, pay more of this, more without saying how, of that.

All such letters would be shortly returned from her vacated, repainted address. No poste restante, as Denise had confirmed. 'Not a chance, love. Not if you knew my mum.' She would clear out completely, then. Dump the lot. It pleased her, this refreshing, tangy thought. There would be nothing, she repeated, hop-scotch like, over the paving stones on the way to the bus stop, nothing for which to return.

Nothing.

The term, which used to abrade her thoughts

like an awkward pill which still asserts its presence after swallowing, was acquiring the ease of oils or sugar-coating. Whatever the reason, perhaps just usage, she no longer minded the two syllables – further, was beginning to find in them an uplift commensurate with fast-acting medicine. *No thing. Nada. Zilch.* For the first time in years she felt a return of religiosity when she attached the concept to herself; felt, as she attempted to sell her last things and walked in farewell around her corner of London, almost as shriven, pure as (she imagined) the possessionless novice. The Buddhism of the seventies had been just a foretaste. *This*, which enabled her soul to feel liberated because it did not yet hurt, was the real thing, the genuine freedom. A clean, eminently movable life without ties or cupidity.

And while, in quiet moments, she admitted that exhilaration may be acting as a pretty kind of varnish, it was largely true that the cupidity had gone. What could she realistically envy? She had passed without noticing the line she had so feared when she had seen others pushed across. She had come so far that it was impossible to covet possessions or envy the possessors; one might as well crave the sketchy appurtenances of distant stars – remote, physical detail one had neither the power nor remaining life span to reach or touch. All that was left to her was to know that somewhere, contained by the lighted windows, stacked hotels, expensive apartment blocks which flanked and bridged her nocturnal walks, luxuries sparkled, more than home comforts warmed. Yet she may never have contact with them again.

Because Elisabet remembered how proud Napoleon had been of her, she had smartened herself up to travel, had mended and washed her clothes and splurged £12 to lighten the hair which had both greyed and darkened. The effect, if not pleasing, was so passable she had no trouble in finding a room. The attic on which she settled, close to the Gare du Nord, because it was both convenient and cheap, looked north, towards the gilded hill of Montmartre. She could just see Sacré Coeur shining against a vivid blue sky on the top, its saline pillars making her think of Lot's wife, who might have turned once, if this were Sodom she were leaving, to look back fondly, regretfully.

As Elisabet learnt more about the area and the reservoir of commercial sex opened around Boulevard Clichy, within view of the chaste sepulchre, and bubbling up, via street transvestites, almost to its foundations, pausing to fester, certainly on the doorstep of a children's school, she came to value greatly her impromptu metaphor. It might not be the most apt, but every morning when, drawing her curtains, she confronted that dome in its isolated radiance, which appeared to focus, as a magnifying-glass, the heat and general beneficence of the sun, she could not help but think of hypocrisy, and that her metaphor was just.

No sun, anyway, reached Elisabet's room except for a rim, a thin, angled slice in mid-morning. For the rest of the day she looked out from darkness to the painted clutter around the church. Actually this symbolism pleased her. She had quickly discovered that, in marked contrast to her first visit, so many years ago, the artists' quarter had smartened up, altered its atmosphere. Some of the houses now looked expensive, while *bijoux* flats had been converted from crumbling *bâtiments*. Despite, or rather along-side, the gaudy tourist shops, in the way that one depradation will propagate and feed others – though each pretends otherwise – it was becoming another fashion-and-notoriety area, a *quartier* whose life mostly consists of that which is ostentatiously done. She preferred the cool detachment of looking up, through her darkness, her shadow, to that sharp, meretricious, but at least foreign, sun.

Well, she could do this for a few days. Unless . . . Lying on her bed to recover from the fatigue of the journey, Elisabet tried to scrape together a sort of plan between dozes. She had intended, originally, to try a little begging every day, in order to finance, perhaps prolong, her stay at the hotel. The young man in the Embankment Gardens had given her to understand she might earn up to £20 *du jour*. With severe economies, she could manage on that.

She knew she was dismissing the fact that she never had managed severe economies except once when, to maintain the intactness of £50, she had refused to buy a vacuum flask. Rashness, spending, as she knew to her cost, is an activity to which the chronically poor are prone, spending to buy a relief which, only for them, is foolish. In inverse proportion, the wealthy and comfortably off do a great deal of it, with impunity. Look, for instance, she told herself as, more wakeful, she began to wonder about tea, at the extravagant afternoon she had spent, when she should have been helping Napoleon in the early spring – ending with a ridiculous lawn handkerchief in Liberty's. She had never even used it – had sold it, eventually, with the rest of her belongings, at a loss. Had sold . . .

But she had promised herself that she would never again think of dispossession, which, in desperation, she had tried to present to herself as a new, cellophane-wrapped, exciting *liberté*. At this lower point in her hotel room, the historical perspective began to show her condition not as some unlooked-for gift or acquisition, but as a punishment, mutilation as stupid, and stupidly wilful, as extravagance; while its roots were so far-reaching as to go beyond her clumsiness with O'Malley, her impoverishing arrogance with her family, as far back as . . ..

Elisabet got up abruptly, straightened her dress, quickly smoothed and reknotted her hair. No more backward glancing. She knew, any fool would know, what darkness, such darkness, like the mouth of an eternal, saturnine tunnel, *that* would open up. Rather, she would concentrate on doing. Immediately that meant, because she was parched, some tea. Yes, sod the cost, she would go out and buy a pot of tea. Tomorrow, which was, thank God, not today, doing meant begging.

But tomorrow held true to its name. However the days passed, it was always the day after this, a condition, or illusion central to sufferers of Micawberism.

Elisabet was no more than a typical case. Tomorrow, as she had agreed with herself, doing meant begging, or otherwise scrounging – she could not yet see how, prostitution, had she the stomach for it, being out. She had seen the competition. Once she had half-heartedly lounged on the wall of the park under Sacré Coeur, but not one man had looked her way, and she had not known what else to do. To begin begging, to set up as a pro, looked equally difficult. Passing the winos who sprawled on

Metro steps and bawled at her for a coin, or the silent North African girls in the tunnels linking different lines, bowing their heads before their begging bowls in a studied, aesthetic fashion, she felt that even here, squatting among strangers, she could not do it. Could not supplicate. The ground, for a start, looked terribly dirty – an overfastidious reaction, but she minded other people's dirt terribly – and the situation of the beggars, who cleverly concealed what success, if any, they had had, appeared so abject. She really thought she preferred the manner of the rougher young Britons, who had shouted obscenities across Hungerford Bridge. Or thought she did.

Anyway, she would do something about it tomorrow; it was only a matter of finding her *métier*, of striking a style, an attitude which, once mastered – she could practise in front of her bedroom mirror – would enable her to take the plunge. She should wear her dirtiest dress, for instance, possibly tearing it here and there; shoeless, stockingless certainly; and with her hair straggling down over her shoulders . . .

Oh, it was all coming together; it was simple, really. She only needed to – study a bit.

Meanwhile – as she did not actually study begging, her thoughts automatically withdrawing from the concept – the good weather continued, hot enough for midsummer. Elisabet did just as she wanted – this is what the sun tells

133

us to do. She walked around central Paris, picking newspapers, etc. from bins (she could not stop the habit now), living, as predicted, on bread and apples with a little cheese, eating her meals in the small, dry, flowerless parks which were hard to find, or sitting on a wall, a flight of steps, looking down at a busy street, or simply walking along among crowds. This foreign French 'busyness' did not disturb her, as, like most tourists, she was easily able to abstract an artistic soul from its midst. Among so many would-bes – painters, novelists, linguists, etc. – tapping, apprentice-like into a culture which seemed so much grander, richer, because it was expressed in a different language, and because they knew only as much of it as invites admiration, Elisabet felt it did not matter, so much, to be poor. It mattered to be bourgeois, perhaps, but it did not matter, so much, to be poor.

It matters more, of course, if there is an endlessness about the state.

Sometimes, in an exercise not unlike masochism, she walked among streets of smarter shops, especially in the Faubourg St Honoré area, where the fashion boutiques amused her; they seemed – were? – so absurd. Looking at the heavily accented, extremely costly, and strangely cut outfits in the windows, at closely stitched and elaborately trimmed leather coats, silk and skin jackets with a sort of in-built musculature at the shoulders, or full sequined dresses in harsh para-primary colours whose taste would be bad were it not that brand labels redeemed them – as if the dictates of certain stylists must invariably be good – she felt, actually, only sorry for the rich, this brand of the, as she put it, narcissistic rich, who must dress like peacocks – even the men, apparently – in order to prove a buying power so easily, in less ugly ways, established.

In fact, most of the devotees, window-gazing like herself, or moving more purposefully along with large, branded carriers, looked not beautiful but risible; as the eyes of many smirking, but more successful *vendeuses* confirmed. Practice, as they say . . .

One comfort. In this street, as in less splendid ones veining south and north, the pain of looking at merchandise she could not afford, at things which wounded again and again, accusing of rank inability, did not apply. The pain came from looking at the people dressed in the merchandise. She herself did not mind not having purchasing power here, not being able to afford even one elaborate handkerchief, whose cost had nothing directly to do with what it was. Was there in fact anything of a more practical and cost-effective nature to be found in these places, should she care or dare to go in?

Hypothetical question, naturally. The fact was, she was not able.

Always with a sense of relief, then, she wandered back into shabbier areas, or on to the fairly democratic gravelled area of the Tuileries, where, sitting on a bench, or in one of the open-air cafés in the low sauterne-coloured sun, she felt herself, like an old flower at the end of the season, preparing to give up. What precious little she had, anyway, if you talk of giving up. Her colour had gone: she was as grey as she was sapless and flaccid. It had been a long time since anyone, she did not mean in the sexual sense, but anyone, for any reason whatever, had given her so much as the flicker of one curious, assessing, and not disparaging glance.

Funnily, she was beginning not to mind that she did not count, the not-minding, like a reaction in the immune system perhaps, having taken not much longer than the noting that one didn't. Sitting on a stone bench under the planes, watching the well-dressed taking their exercise, she wondered into what bracket she could fit, supposing she could climb back into the social structure, which is only, she thought, a large wall of hanging brackets, and more fixed than you might think. She was not talking about illusion; she was talking of actuality, one which included that noisy room in Victoria from which she had been evicted, and to which she did not want to return. In a way the eviction seemed to her like a kindness, a reminder that all stages end. That ending had precipitated her here, which she would not have missed for the world.

Suddenly sentimental tears filled her. She wept, a little, for a nation which had not seemed to care for such as her, or, to put it another way, a society whose brackets had *all* been unaccommodating – even the one into which she had been born – like sets of garments made for different figures, none of them her type. Made, for instance, for artisans, manual workers, the housewife as much as the hustler, the high-flier, above all, she said, the already monied or landed people. Poor Elisabet had failed with her novels, those weighty manuscripts she had abstracted from how much of life, which she had hoped would express just something of her otherwise wasted existence, and which she had dumped, two weeks ago, in someone else's rubbish bin. She had failed in her jobs, her relationships, failed in each area attempted, each avenue, sub-bracket and bracket. Everything so fixed, so determinedly described! She had failed, at the last, with Napoleon, who had always said, because of the kindness which had filled her face (or was it the plumpness of turning fifty; or that constitutional vagueness so often confused with a tender heart?), that she should have had a family, a large, sprawling, difficult, multi-talented family. Whom she should have watched, sitting on a Skye beach, writing letters . . .

She could have had . . . there were hundreds of items in thousands of permutations. But at the last she hadn't. She had kept on not having, in an ever-declining scale, until here she was, feeling, as she experienced them, memories draining out of her that she never wanted to remember again. Neither those, nor the pain of what they evoked or meant. She seemed to be remembering everything as if for the last time, every good or interesting thing which she had done (there weren't many!), every situation, event, person who had struck a note – they struck their notes again, struck from her a subtle, partial tone, as if she were a bell, or gong, capable of many irregular, idiosyncratic notes. The memories stirred within and, rising, materialising, roused such plangent vibrations from bench, wall or café chair, she visibly shuddered. They were changed memories, of course, better and more poignant; they knew how to play their instrument to maximum effect. But even so, just as soon as they had sounded, they began to fade. One note succeeds another. The tune runs forward. The musician turns over a page. While Elisabet, performing, responding, her own enclosed event, went on for hours. For days.

Once she thought that this was how you must

feel when dying. And then she was sure that it was, because, as her last francs trickled away, like leaking, poor-quality blood, she felt that the force that was her spirit – which used to seem a plucky if not indomitable spirit, but which was now tired, exhausted, had given up – wanted to drain away. There was no fight, no resistance left. And so she let the memories flow, escape. She felt them touch, resonate and leave. That was their end, she said, and felt that largely, though melodramatic, she was right. For they would not be communicated to another soul nor, if she could help it, ever again be entertained. This is the essential sadness of the unremarkable, failed life.

Sometimes, at night, listening to drunks passing in the street, Elisabet wished she had enough spunk to scream with frustration, to make a scene, to swallow anaesthesia every night as these voluble men were doing. (She detected no female voice.) She envied them, or at least their wholehearted embrace of such catalysts – alcohol, drugs, company – as mimic or temporarily make up for change. But she could not join in. Or not yet. She recalled Napoleon. Strangely, she was beyond interest in drink.

And then, the day came when her money ran out.

She had, when trying to envisage it, thought there would be spectacular scenes, arguments, accusations, leading to the calling of the police. In the event, displacement was as quiet as her self-eviction from Victoria, as all the other events of her life, with the exception of the tussle with O'Malley. Her wish for unobtrusiveness and a fund of good manners won over the brief assertion, the kickback which did not survive, of a spirit that wished her to make a mark, for she might never again have the opportunity.

In fact, the whole thing was so much of the opposite nature as to be absurd. She had a bill at the hotel which she paid with the sum she had set aside. She had lasted just over two weeks, longer than anticipated, having done what extremity had pushed her to and stolen a handbag some woman had placed on a bench before turning to gossip with a friend. Elisabet, almost at the end of such savings as were left, after deducting rent, did not regret the act as a crime – no more than revolutionaries regard execution as a legal offence. It is (arguably) necessary, and the pain (Elisabet had weighed up the woman's accessories nicely) to the victim short.

There were almost 1,500 francs in a wad of hundreds and fifties in the bag. That had cushioned wonderfully for another ten days. At the end of which she could, of course, have stayed on in her room; she had paid a deposit on arriving, they may not fuss for some time. But it had never been her intention to moonlight, for all sorts of reasons: prudence, reticence, compassion – those hampering good manners. She actually liked the people who ran the hotel. They kept the room clean, were modest, did not press her for cash. If she robbed again, she would rather take from those who could better afford it.

Then there was the prospect of being caught – easy when you are homeless – and, for all she knew, deportation, which she would vigorously avoid. London was now out. For preference, she thought, she would beg among the slipping decay of Venice, or on the old Christian battle-grounds of Rome. But Paris was acceptable. Paris would do. Besides, there comes a time, as she decided on her final night, when the inevitable is so close you must hurry or, at the least, not decline to embrace it. Packing her light travel bag in the morning – so light now, so weightless – lingering by the window with the sunlit church right of centre, Elisabet welcomed, as one might the twist of a resolute spring, the fact that the last move was in the way of being accomplished. She was on the way to meet it; no more deflections, she had made the decision. It was much like going to the dentist, the experience of which begins when one is *en route*, long before the waiting-room, the expectant chair. For one has chosen that path, and with decision lives, always, though often submerged, knowledge of its effects. Only the deceitful claim otherwise – claim that they did not know.

Elisabet had known for years. And while this denouement may have been deferred, it was a mark of her novel resolution that, rather than prevaricate, she preferred to know exactly what, how little, how uncomfortable, the outcome of her life was going to be. Neither was this apathy, haste, call it what you will, a peculiar trait: she had noticed it in many others, among friends of Napoleon and so on. It was like drowning, possibly – ineluctable and, at a certain stage, irresistible, a slow fall through an unaccommodating social structure. She had been falling for decades. She knew exactly what falling was; it was not unlike and no less alarming than sliding quickly, if bumpily, down the pencilled axis on some graph. She only wanted to complete the process by touching bottom. Then she would have experienced everything. As far as the statistician was concerned, she would be almost off the page, understanding all but signifying nothing.

Which was not so much a question of bravery as of inevitability. Or perhaps it was brave in the beginning. Perhaps it had been brave not to resist her landlord; unless that acquiescence was only a function of being tired? Yes, she was very tired, tired and quite hopeless as she stood in the tidied room with her bag before descending to pay. She

thought again of Napoleon, of his fatigue, his
disbelief that anything would ever get any
better, and saw that what she had feared there,
but denied would come to her, had settled
already on her shoulders. They had rounded too;
she no longer held her back straight, as the
wardrobe mirror confirmed. She was stooped,
tidy but dreary, and there was something a little
off-centre, crabwise . . . O God, she said, turning
quickly and picking up her bag. Abruptly the
door rattled, opened, was closed. Beside it,
quivering a little from the impact, all the mirror
in the armoire against the window showed (as if
it had seen, but promised to keep her secret) was
what it had shown, implacably, in different
places for 200 years: a long streak of shadow
gashed, here and there, with some images of
fixtures and small uncertainties of light.

'*Au revoir, Madame. Au revoir.*' The proprietor
could not appreciate the significance of his
remark as he ushered her from the warm lobby
into the fresher street. Overnight a light wind
had sprung up, and she did actually, though she
might have done this symbolically, shiver. Had
the small group who watched her go noticed this
– guessed anything? It would have been interesting to see herself through their eyes. She
had, or thought she had, until that moment
upstairs, made herself neater for the occasion,
pulling her hair into a more formal, less escapist,

bun, while her dress was passably clean. She could have been any dowdy woman making an insignificant journey; perhaps they would remark nothing except something resigned in her bearing. But to Elisabet it seemed that, in leaving the hotel, she was not only abandoning final territory, but at last crossing the margins of herself as an ordinary person. It was a moment of the greatest significance, and it was therefore a pity that, as in christenings, confirmations, marriages, and certain kinds of death, there was no camera to record the event.

The day passed in a fairly ordinary manner. She walked about, increasingly irritated by the weight of her bag. She stole some small items from a supermarket, bought bread, and ate them. In the early evening, she used the public lavatories and washing facilities at Gare du Nord. She still looked decent enough for these, or a café; but wondered how long that would last.

Then she sat on one of the moulded seats on the station concourse watching passers-by. Time passed, and still she watched, admiring how purposeful and energetic they seemed. Everyone with somewhere to go! It was dark outside, and because of the wind, colder today. She had made no plans about where to spend the night; dossers should mark their pitches early, but she had made no such move. It seemed somehow ridiculous, and pathetic, that she should. Why bother? Anywhere would do. The risks were all the same.

Towards 10 p.m. her eyes began to close. She wedged her bag behind her and, turning in the seat, rested her head. It was not awfully comfortable, but you should expect that. Someone would move her on eventually, but she might doze undisturbed for an hour. She must remember, though, the little ritual that she had decided to repeat each night before sleeping, and again on waking. She remembered that once, long ago, there had been some nonsense about finding a vocabulary to encompass loss. In fact, you did not find it. The words emerged of their own: plain, ordinary, mostly one-syllable words, the words that describe where you will sleep, how you feel, and what you will eat today. They were not palliative, but accepting. They did not help, they only told. They were almost as solid and unattractive as the objects and concepts they named: bench, drink, shit, fear.

Eventually, these words would not be used any more. They would be absorbed by automatic impulses. They would be the terms that others used for what one did. So why, Elisabet asked, should she bother with her little ritual: her name, birth date, today's date, the year? She looked up at the starless dirt on the station's roof. She felt dirty particles stirring in the draught beneath her seat, and felt that draught communicating, soul-lessly, with all the places she must drag herself to, and lie down in, and be moved on from, as if she were no more than a leaf being buffeted about, bruised against those very buildings where others slept in peace.

And then it seemed that rituals have no power against this nightmare. They cannot, however you look at it, matter in this unordinary world to which the homeless are jettisoned as if they are no more than rats – though, actually, rats fare better. To what could she compare it, now that she wished she had not been so foolish as to pursue her fate? Underworld? Concentration camps – Buchenwald, Auschwitz? Or – what did they call them – killing fields? Horrors that only time or other distances render admissable. She could see herself, for instance, in a snap looked at some twenty years on.

'Poor thing', would be the comment. Perhaps a negative of Napoleon already waited in some file.

But now the wind in the station entrance was rising, whistling obscenities between columns. Elisabet shivered. Her lips moved, but she did not repeat her mantra. Then someone passing stopped at a safe distance to stare. She looked back, but the man did not flinch, or seem to mind. It was almost as if he were watching theatre. While in fact he was not seeing at all, not seeing what pity or curiosity had arranged, for the present moment, into passable matter. It was only herself who had learnt that to feel is the same as to see. The other is only blindness.

Eventually the man stepped forward and held out two coins. She did not move, so he placed them on her crumpled lap. Then she watched him swing about and walk towards the station exit as once, she supposed, Napoleon had watched her turn and walk towards the safety of home, anxious to forget her sketchy idea of what he felt, anxious to believe that numbness covered and eased his wounds.

Well, probably it had not. Not then. It was too early, as it was for herself. The clock registered 22.13. Her eyes were heavy. The two coins lay in her lap. It was cold and the bag bit into the back of her head as fiercely as the manacles of some trap. Eventually her hand moved to cover the coins. They were thin and light. They had been gratuitous, unsolicited, but they were her first *cache. So you can do it*, she said. And it seemed not marvellous at all; it seemed only correct that against her tremendous fear she could comfort her palm with this stranger's gift, which he had placed in her lap like an offering at a shrine. Had she moved him, then? Had she, as never in her life before, embodied something with her plight?

Certainly, there was a something here, a start. Though Elisabet did not yet know how to go on from this beginning. Soon she ceased thinking about it as, rocking, mumbling, forgetting to speak just inwardly to herself, moving her hand caressingly, obsessively, over her two thin coins, she looked, as far as a few passers-by were concerned, with her bag at her neck and a white plastic carrier at her feet, almost content.